Finding Faith

A Dragon's Fated Heart book 2

Paranormal Romance

By Beverly Ovalle

Beverly Ovalle

If you still don't care that you got it free from a pirate site, at least have the decency to leave a review!

Beverly Ovalle

Finding Faith

Copyright © 2019 Beverly Ovalle

First E-book Publication: May 2019

ISBN 978-0-9967-9738-2

Cover design by JM Walker

Edited by Molly S Daniels

All cover art and logo copyright © 2019 by Beverly Ovalle

TABLE OF CONTENTS

Beverly Ovalle

Dedication:

This past year I lost my best friend, Tamara Hoffa. I can't help but cry while I write this. We weren't just Facebook friends or author friends. (Check out her books online!) We went to high school together. Tam lived at my house while her parents moved so she didn't have her school interrupted while they found a house and got settled. Then she joined them. Our friendship stayed strong even though she moved from Illinois to Florida. Even when the years passed and we had minimal contact. Even when I was sailing around the world. We always picked up where we left off.

Somewhere there is a photo of us making snow angels in our pajamas. I think it was something like thirty degrees out. Another of me wearing a god-awful dress (it was the 80's) standing up in her wedding to Michael. She, of course, looked beautiful.

Her memory brings tears to my eyes and a smile to my face. Before all the texting started, we had our own acronyms. SSLY was one we've used since high school. Smile Somebody Loves You.

And I'll love you forever. Be at peace my friend. We'll catch up again one day.

PROLOGUE

Crag leaned over, snagging a little piece of pink cloth from the floor. Clenching his fist, he lifted it to his nose, the scent assaulting his nostrils. Inhaling, the spiciness pervaded his lungs, curling inside of him, clenching his gut. Snapping his eyes open, Crag breathed in the scent in again, savoring it. His dick twitched. Lowering his hand, he gazed at the delicate panties. The scent assuring him they belonged to his mate. Lifting them again to his nose, he took another deep sniff, enjoying the spicy bouquet and imprinting the scent of his mate forever onto his soul.

He turned at the gasp behind him. Hope, his brother's mate looked at him in disgust.

"Is that necessary?"

His lips twitched. "Her scent is strongest in what she wore closest to her body." He raised his brow, daring her to argue with him.

"Hmpf." Hope shook her head and gestured for him to leave the room. "Just find my sister."

Crag shoved the pink panties in his pocket. He didn't need them, but he wanted them. Pleased with having something of his mate's, he quirked a grin at Hope. Patting Hope on the head he turned and left. The growl from her was just a bit of icing on the cake. Crag shook his head passing Hope's grandmother. The twitch of his lips the only sign of his amusement.

"Monster."

She sidled past, the whispered word whipping his head toward her. His low growl sent her gasping, escaping into the room he'd just vacated.

He hoped the grandmother wasn't going to be a problem.

CHAPTER ONE

Faith shoved a tree limb out of her way, a thrill of satisfaction weaving through her at the distance she'd travelled from home. Pushing through the dense forest, ignoring the snap of branches whipping in her face, Faith forged forward. Yanked to a standstill, Faith tugged at her satchel snagged on a low hanging branch. With a crack, it pulled it free. She couldn't leave it behind, caught in a tree. It carried the few necessities she needed for survival. Nothing would stop her, not even the branches trying to hold her in place.

She knew, in her heart, her soul, she was meant for something else. She was determined to find another town, and another, moving until she knew where she belonged. Staring at the sky peeking through the trees, Faith smiled. Her heart raced, excited to be following her dreams.

She had a plan to gain acceptance anywhere she went. Looking around, spying the nearby plants, she grinned triumphantly. They were planted evenly, if a bit wild and overgrown. A leftover garden from years ago.

A long-ago house evident in the rubble left in corners of what once was a foundation.

A healer was always welcome. The only strangers that hadn't been chased out of their town were healers and herbalists. She'd learned everything she could from them. Plants and their properties always fascinated her.

She needed to be prepared. Her chest lightening, her dreams in sight, Faith headed toward the nearest patch of herbs. She might as well start collecting now. She didn't know where or what plants grew away from here. Here she knew. She'd tried to put them in order, weeding and saving what she could identify from the old books in the remains of the library.

Sunlight dappled the ground, weaving in and out of the branches. Spilling out its brilliance onto the leaves. Faith breathed deep, the scent of the pines making the air crisp in the early morning chill. Slowly gathering a variety of herbs, Faith went from one patch to another, heading farther away from home. Carefully preserving the plants to the roots. Once she found where she was going, she would plant them and hope they would grow.

Finding Faith

She straightened, twisting to relieve the pain in her back from picking plants. Taking a deep breath, Faith looked around her and squared her shoulders. She hadn't been this way often, but she was still within easy distance from home. Too close to tarry much longer.

Heading deeper into the trees, Faith forced her way through the forest, pushing branches out of her way. Ignoring the scratches they left behind. The scent of dirt and the faintly musty scent of decaying leaves filled her nostrils. Life. Freedom. Adventure. Everything she wanted. She bounced on the balls of her feet. Excitement filling her soul.

The trees let minimal sunlight through, keeping the area cool. The leaves varied in dappled shades of green. Filling her lungs with fresh air, a shiver raced down her spine. Faith relaxed, a smile teasing her lips. The blue peeking through the leaves lightening her heart.

With her shoulders back, Faith strode forward. She would find her own way. Follow a path not prescribed by her family. Find what her soul was crying out for.

Following a faint trail, Faith realized she was heading toward the meadow she and Hope had recently been to. They'd laid traps and snares out, hoping to catch rabbits to restock their colony. Hope was trying to snare a few white ones for shoes their aunt promised to make her.

Her tummy growled. Hmm. Maybe one was already filled. A diet of trail mix wasn't appealing, though it would do. She'd grab the snare too. Empty or not, she'd have one to trap game along her journey.

Inching her way to the closest one, Faith was thrilled to see it held a rabbit. Faith pulled it from the snare. Draping it over a nearby branch, Faith quickly grabbed the trap, wrapping it up and stashing it in her satchel.

Skinning the rabbit, careful to keep the skin intact, she laid it on the largest leaves she could find. Sprinkling some rosemary on it, Faith wrapped the leaves around the meat. She tucked it in the outside of her satchel. She needed to keep moving. If anyone was out hunting and saw a fire, they would join her then expect her to return with them. So, a little farther along and she'd feel safer from being found.

Circling the outside of the meadow, staying hidden in the trees, Faith headed farther from home and away from any recognizable path.

Hopefully no one would realize she was gone until tomorrow.

Her eyes widened at the snarl of a big cat. Faith froze. The sounds of the forest stopped. The cry changed to a snarl of pain. Faith crept beneath a tree, hiding from sight beneath its branches. Curious, she moved silently, trying to peek into the meadow. She gasped.

A shadow flew overhead, darkening the grass of the meadow. A large cat dangling from its claws.

Faith gasped, stunned. It couldn't be. Fairy tales depicted them, showing the devastation they caused. She stared, heart thundering. Hidden beneath the drooping branches of a pine, she was invisible from the sky. A second one swooped down, snatching its prey and flying away. Faith shrank back then froze. The scream echoing through the woods was all too familiar. It faded, more and more distant as the dragon stole away his prey.

Her breath caught, her heart stuttering. Oh no, it was Hope! Faith couldn't help but recognize her own sister's voice. Frozen, she stared, watching the monsters fly away.

Shaking her head, tightening her lips, she scrambled forward. She had to rescue Hope. There wasn't time to go home for help. Sliding her knife in her belt, she ran, taking care to stay out of sight in the trees. Crossing the meadow might be shorter, but even though the dragons carried away one cougar, Faith couldn't chance it. Solitary animals, if the cougar had young nearby, it wouldn't be safe. She was no match against even a baby. No use becoming a meal through carelessness.

No matter how long it took, she would follow. Hope would do the same for her. Thoughts of finding a new life fell away. She had to save her sister.

CHAPTER TWO

The wind lifted his wings. The pressure had him making small unconscious adjustments with his muscles to glide easily through the sky. The soothing touch against his crest and down his back felt like fingers touching him all over. Crag loved nothing more than flying. Well, and eating, he loved eating.

He glanced over at his brother Ari and his new mate Hope. He shook his head. Crag ignored them despite wanting to smile at Hope's behavior. He flew ahead, scouting out the territory. Crag just wanted to make sure it was safe. Hope dived and swirled, enjoying the feel of the air against her wings if her smile was anything to go by.

They'd persuaded him to stay another night at Hope's. Growling and glaring he regretted his decision to stay immediately. He managed to aggravate everyone around him. So much, they urged him to leave before darkness blanketed the town. Finally. Then, Ari and Hope decided to follow. Of course, his other brothers, Rog and Hark wouldn't be left behind either.

17

Their decision to follow him, hoping to find Faith aggravated him just a little bit. Did they think he couldn't find her by himself? Her essence imprinted on his soul, giving him no other needed incentive to find her. Remembering the scent from her panties had his dick growing. Flying with a stiffy could get painful. He moved away from Ari. He didn't need to be teased.

"Aren't you two ready to go back?" He wished they would turn around. He didn't want them looking for his mate with him. It felt too personal. Even if it was Ari and his mate's sister. Brother and new sister, but still. Somehow, he knew he needed to find Faith on his own.

"Don't you want our company?" Ari flashed laughing eyes in his direction.

Ass. Crag growled.

Ari just smirked. "Fine. We'll leave you alone." He turned his head toward his mate. "Hope, let's go back to your parents' home."

Crag rolled his eyes. Hope was swooping and diving, enjoying her new-found freedom to fly. Ignoring her mate. Typical. She'd been a handful since Ari stole her away.

Ari took off after her, herding her back the way they'd come.

Hope's laughter tinkling across the sky.

Crag wondered if Faith was a spitfire like her sister.

He wondered what Faith looked like. Would she have autumn tresses like Hope? Dainty like her mother or sturdy like her father? Raven haired or pale like the top of wheat fields? Maybe a mix in between. No one had mentioned it. He growled. It was a good thing he could hunt her by scent and the tugging of his heart.

Crag's eyes roved through the trees. He was hungry. Sometimes he felt that he was always hungry. He could feel the rumble in his stomach. His nostrils flared. He could smell prey but didn't have time to stop. There were more important things to do.

He had felt the urge to fly north much as Ari. Ari's instincts had led him to Hope. Glad for his brother, but Crag still had that urge to keep moving. Only this time it was sending him south.

Meeting Hope's family, following her home, he'd found the scent of his mate. Now it appeared to be dragging him home. No one knew where Faith had gone. Crag wondered why she had left. Only time would tell.

"Bye." Hope's voice was almost indistinct. She and Ari quickly flew back the way they'd come, turning into specks in the sky.

He worried about their safety with Hope's family. Crag didn't trust that grandmother of Hope's. A warning to Ari seemed appropriate. Especially since he wouldn't be there to have his brother's back.

Be careful of the grandma.

I will. But with Hope on my side, I should be able to win her over.

Don't be arrogant. If she attempts to harm us, I'll have to dispose of her.

It won't come to that.

We'll see.

Crag hoped Ari took him seriously. Most humans couldn't be trusted. Look at what they had done to each other. Of course, it was to the dragons' advantage. They now were able to fly again without worry of being found out. Even if they were seen, the humans could do nothing about it. They'd reduced themselves back to their primitive beginnings.

Crag itched to see the rest of the world. It would be wonderful to safely fly anywhere he wanted to go.

Sometime in the future Hope's family might know what they were. Right now, the dragons were safer not informing them. Especially with one of them hostile, regardless of her age. Crag would never underestimate a human.

Are you sure she's really your mate? Ari spoke up.

I'm sure.

Absolutely, positively? Now Rog was joining in. Great.

Yes. Now do something useful and leave me alone.

Call if you need help. Ari spoke, hopefully for the last time.

Yes, like if you need to change your mate when you find her. Rog and Hark's snickers echoed through their connection. All four of them had been necessary to change Hope. They all arrived with Ari, bringing Hope home at her demand before Ari took her away again to their Weyr. Now all of them followed him. Hopefully his brothers followed Ari back.

Crag ground his teeth. He'd always been possessive. The fact that he would need his brothers to change his mate stuck in his craw. Ari said that once the mating heat hit, nothing bothered him except getting more of his mate. He hoped that was true. He'd hate to have to kill his brothers.

Not that he didn't want that most of the time anyway. Hark and Rog were the jokesters of the family. His two brothers tumbled in and out of trouble, trying their best to be the bane of his existence. Crag grumbled. To be honest, not just his. They pranked all of them equally.

Be careful. Let me know if you need us. And Ari called Crag the worrywart.

I will. Don't let your mate lead you around by your nose.

As if. I have other things for her to grab.

Crag snickered. Ari was lucky Hope hadn't figured out how to talk mind to mind yet. He'd have to watch his mouth then. His feisty little mate would be looking for his balls and it wouldn't be to play with.

If he was lucky, his brothers would return with Ari and Hope instead of continuing to follow him. But he wouldn't count on it.

Crag flew on. The silence was welcome after being in the human compound. His stomach rumbled once again. Spying a disturbance on the ground, he circled, landing to check it out.

He found evidence of a small fire and blood. Sniffing, his stomach rumbled. Rabbit and Faith permeated the area. Shifting, Crag poked at the fire. It was cold. Crag frowned. He wondered where Faith was headed and why.

He followed, frowning. Broken limbs attested to her passage.

Crag decided to follow on foot. Faith had gone through the forest, not following a path, but making her own. With the heavier coverage overhead, he would have lost her trail. He debated changing into his dragon but decided it would be easier to follow Faith as a man.

The trail continued. He wasn't small in his human form and Faith's path followed no rhyme or reason that he could see, not to mention, the tight passage was uncomfortable. Growling, Crag changed, his dragon cracking branches while he fought his way back to the sky.

He would just fly over the tree tops. Hmm, no, that's not what he would do. Grinning in anticipation, he decided to fly *through* the tree tops. The trees scraping his sides and belly while he flew, his width clearing out any dead branches, and sending them crashing to the ground sounded like heaven to his ears. Crag sighed in pleasure, flying as low as he could. The brush and bark scratching itches he normally couldn't reach, and his excess skin sloughing off as he flew. Soon enough, the scent of his mate wound through his senses.

He felt the urging in his soul and his heart had no choice but to follow the path fate had set for him. Accepting it, Crag followed. He would find her faster flying than fighting his way in the undergrowth behind her.

His stomach rumbled, making him aware of his hunger. Crag decided a meal was in order. He rose above the tree tops, searching for something big enough to sate his appetite. He spied a small tributary and plenty of game. He could afford a small stop. He travelled twice as fast as Faith did on foot. Flying, he'd find her in no time at all.

The river looked inviting and he could eat to his heart's content and still find his mate. His urgency expended, Crag assumed his mate was near, her scent was too fresh for her not to be. She needed to eat and sleep and it would only make sense for her to camp here for the night.

Crag pumped his wings, rising high. Turning, he slid into the air currents that would take him faster with less effort to where he wanted to go. His heart lightened, the intense blue of the sky soothing his edginess. Crag drew a deep breath, released a roar, a smirk edging his lips. It was good to be alive.

Movement below him caught his eye. Crag tipped, the drag on his wings slowing him down enough to allow him to circle.

Crag skimmed the trees, looking to see any movement. With a huff, he rose. Nothing. He reared back, arrowing higher into the sky. Hunting a creature in the trees was unnecessary when easier prey was to be found. The only creature in the trees would be his mate.

Mentally marking the location, Crag circled, gliding in the current.

The wind blew against his scales, ruffling the row of spikes running down his back. His wings pumped once, twice, and a third time, propelling Crag high into the sky. Crag stretched in the cooler temperatures. Shivering, and gaining speed to stir his blood. Today was a good day.

Spiraling in the currents, Crag maneuvered, the wind warmed against his wings the closer he flew to the earth.

Focusing on the plodding movements of the herd below, Crag slowed. No need to stampede them. He would chase them if he had to but preferred a quick snatch and run.

Gliding in, Crag grabbed a cow from the edge of the herd. His talons pierced the tough hide. The agonized lowing spurred the rest of the animals into a run. Settling down in the emptying field, Crag bit down. The crunch of bones echoed across the clearing with each bite and warm blood filled his stomach, quieting the grumble. He hummed, finishing off his prey in short order. A belch relieved him. Licking his talons, Crag sniffed the air.

Crag rose, ponderously making his way to the water. Dipping his claws in, he wiggled them in the silt at the bottom of the river. He leaned forward and drank. Drawing deep mouthfuls, to wash down his meal.

He slid into the water, rolling in the soft sandy bottom of the river. Rubbing his scales along the bottom to reach that one particular spot that itched. It was too shallow to submerge fully. Crag slid, washing each part of his body. Standing in the water, Crag shook, and crawled partially into the grass, leaving the rest of his body in the stream.

"Mmmm." Sprawling half in and half out of the water, Crag settled down. The warm sun on his back had his second eyelids closing. The lap of the water against his belly and the soft feel of the mud between his talons soothed him. A sigh escaped.

The buzzing of bees, the trill of birds surrounded him. A deep breath wafted a sweet smell to his nostrils. Crag relaxed, imaging the smell of his mate surrounded him. He slid a bit down on the bank, wiggling in the water. Her scent seemed to fill his nostrils. Crag

27

rumbled, feeling himself harden, glad of the coolness of the water. He arched forward, the mud beneath the edge of the water encompassing his cock. It felt good. Groaning he pulled back, the suction of the mud teasing him.

Fuck it. Crag kept his head down, eyes closed and humped the edge of the river. The mud was soft enough for him to penetrate but sticky enough to suck him back in. If felt damn good. With the scent of his mate in his nose, Crag imagined plunging into her. Humping faster and faster, he shot his wad into the mud with a growl. Pulling free from the mud, he raised his ass into the air, swished his cock in the river to rinse the mud from it. Settling back down, his body cushioned, Crag relaxed.

Crag could smell the flowery scent of his mate. It soothed the beast inside him. He wondered what his mate would be like. He was sure she'd be perfect for him. With a sigh, he slid into slumber.

CHAPTER THREE

Her stomach rumbled. The rabbit had only lasted a couple of days. Faith hadn't seen any more evidence of dragons so she kept heading in the direction they flew. Her stomach rebelling, the ache called for something more substantial than her trail mix.

Aware she couldn't hold her own against any predators, Faith set up a camp underneath the sweeping branches of a large pine far enough away from the water to hopefully be safe. The limbs weighed down, creating a cozy little den without any effort on her part. She cleared an area of pine needles, digging down into the dirt. She could safely start a fire now. Her mouth watered, imagining the juices of a freshly roasted rabbit.

Crawling out from her shelter, her next plan was setting up her snare. She could hear a stream nearby. She should be able to hunt there. Water would definitely attract game. She'd set up her snare and hope that she could get at least one animal. Rabbit, squirrel, it didn't matter. She needed fresh meat.

Turning she headed toward the sound of water. Watching the signs for smaller game trails, Faith blew out a breath when she identified one. Quickly setting the snare, she headed to the river. Hopefully she would catch something soon. In the meantime, she'd refill her canteen and maybe get a bath in. She glanced up at a roar, the sight stilling her heart. A dragon!

Stunned she watched the dragon fly overhead. It circled back around. She froze, hiding beneath the overhanging branches of a pine. Then it was gone again. Faith looked at the sky, making sure it was clear and ran. Towards the dragon. Shaking her head, Faith knew she must be crazy. There couldn't be that many of them. This one had to have been one of the two who'd stolen Hope. She followed it. Hopefully her sister was here.

The trees cleared suddenly. Faith stopped, winded. Hiding behind a tree, she watched the dragon finish off a cow. The rest of the herd were as far away as they could get, lowing in distress. Faith imagined she'd be upset too if one of her family was being devoured by the dragon.

Faith froze and swallowed. Shaking her head, she forced the thought away. Hope had been alive when they'd taken her. She still had to be alive. Judging the size of the cow the dragon was chomping away on, Hope would barely have been a snack.

She crept closer, trying to stay hidden behind a tree trunk. The dragon stood and began plodding toward the river. Faith stifled a laugh. She had always imagined them to be more graceful. The dragon's belly practically scraped the ground. Faith had followed the river through the woods, knowing she needed the water and the fish it provided for food. If she could catch any.

Faith watched the dragon gambol in the river. There was the grace it was missing on the ground. He really was magnificent. It. No, no way could she start thinking of it as anything other than an animal. Though she couldn't help but notice it was male. The dragon crawled up the bank, relaxing, sprawled half in and half out of the water. She watched it move.

Faith frowned wondering what was wrong with it. Her eyes widened, her jaw dropping. It was definitely male. He was humping the water. A snicker escaped. Faith clamped her hands over her mouth, trying not to be heard. His scales gleamed in the sun, flashing with each buck into the water. Black with green tints. His haunch moved faster and faster until it, no, he, no, it, growled, shaking.

Faith smothered her chuckles, tears stinging her eyes. She swallowed as he raised in the water, his cock rocking back and forth until no mud was left. It was huge. Bigger than any bulls she'd seen. Definitely bigger than any horses also.

She watched as he lay back down in the water and settled into slumber. Goodness, she couldn't believe he'd humped the water. Wait until she found Hope and told her. They would both laugh. Faith sobered, her eyes widening. She would kill the dragon if he had harmed her sister.

Faith crept closer, a noise from the dragon stilling her in her tracks. She wrinkled her nose at the bubbles rising in the water behind it. The popping began and Faith plugged her nose and tried not to gag. Eyes watering, she hurried as far away from the dragon as she could. Faith tripped and fell forward into the dirt, a shriek falling from her lips.

Taking a deep breath, she pushed herself up trying to stay quiet. The bottoms of her hands stung. She didn't have time to worry about it. She couldn't be caught. Heavens knew what would happen to her. She glanced back at the Dragon. It hadn't roused. Faith looked at what she had tripped over. She frowned. Glancing from the dragon to the sack, she swallowed.

Oh God, he did eat people. The sack must have been caught on his talons or perhaps looped around one of those sharp teeth that filled his mouth. She shuddered. Grabbing the strap, Faith pulled it toward her. She couldn't see any blood. With it in her hands Faith stood. Maybe something in the sack would tell her who it belongs to. Once she found Hope she would try to find the family of the missing stranger to let them know what happened to him. Faith couldn't imagine never knowing what happened to Hope.

Faith heard a noise behind her and broke into a run. She would hide in the trees and hope the dragon couldn't find her there. She thought she heard wings. Gasping a lungful of air, Faith tried to move faster.

"Where do you think you're going with my clothes?"

Faith whirled around. "Look out for…" The dragon was gone. He must've had no interest in her or hadn't seen her. She sagged in relief, looking into the sky. "Did you see that? Where did it go?"

The stranger walked toward her. "I don't know what you're talking about. But I would appreciate my sack back."

Faith lowered her eyes, looking at the man coming towards her. Her cheeks turned hot, her tummy tingling. The man was strikingly handsome and totally nude. Faith sucked in a mouthful of air, staring.

He walked closer seemingly unconcerned with his state of undress. He held his hand out. "That is mine."

Faith just stared at his groin. She swallowed, her mouth dry. She couldn't tear her eyes away. She watched his cock rise, thickening with each step. She stepped forward. Reaching out her hand, she grasped the hard smoothness. His heat had her jumping back, realizing what she had done.

"Oh my God." Faith lowered her eyes. Her cheeks burned, the heat filling even her ears in shame. The unfamiliar tingling in her panties shook her. "I'm so sorry. I've never done such a thing before."

He chuckled and grabbed her hand. "Here, feel free." He wrapped her hand around his length. His hand covered hers moving it in an up-and-down motion.

It was hard but soft. Faith tightened her hand, staring down. He groaned, and tightened his hand over hers, speeding the motion up. Dropping the bag Faith grasped him with both hands. His skin moved freely up and down his pole. Heat pooled in her belly, an unfamiliar ache in her pussy made her clench her legs together.

She slid a finger over the top of his dick. The cap was soft with a small indentation. A drop of warm cream spilled down her fingers. Faith touched it marveling at the softness. Another drop welled up, following the same path. With a swipe, she gathered it up on her fingertip, placing it in her mouth.

"Are you trying to unman me?"

Faith looked at him in confusion. "What?"

"Nothing."

"I'm sorry." Faith shook her head and tried to step back, loosening her hands. "I don't know what's gotten into me."

He grabbed her hands, tightening them around him. "Don't let go. It feels good."

Faith's eyes widened. "I shouldn't." Her nipples were tight, begging to be touched. She wouldn't glance down to see if they were betraying her desire. She could feel the slickness and the heat that gathered in her sex. No man had ever affected her like this.

"I won't tell. There's no one around to see." He thrust his hips, slipping through her fingers.

Faith tightened them. She wanted this. He pulled her closer. "Did you like the taste?"

Faith swallowed and nodded. "Yes." She knew she shouldn't admit that. Who knows what the stranger might do to her?

He groaned. "You could lick it." At his words she felt him thicken and surge forward.

Faith cast her eyes down. Running her tongue over her lips she imagined the salty flavor on her tongue. "May I?" She whispered it so softly Faith was surprised he heard her.

"In a moment." He slid his hands inside the front of her pants sliding fingers against her sensitive core.

He rubbed her clit for a moment before sliding a finger into her body.

Faith shook and sucked in a breath. She gasped, shivering. His rough finger felt strange but thrilling penetrating her swollen sex. She clenched, bucking against him.

"I want to see what you taste like too." He pulled his hand out of her pants and slipped it into his mouth. "Like ambrosia." He flashed a crooked grin at her.

Heat filled her cheeks. Faith exhaled harshly at his actions. His golden eyes gleamed at her. She had no idea why he was affecting her like this. But she couldn't seem to turn away. Even thoughts of the dragon no longer concerned her. Her sex grasped at air, missing the thickness of his finger. She wondered what it would be like to have him penetrate her, his long cock filling the space she hadn't realized begged to be filled.

He pushed down on her shoulders until she was on her knees in front of him. His large member bobbed in front of her face. She grasped it, watching another milky tear escape. Faith leaned forward, and licked it up, moaning at the salty flavor bursting on her tongue.

She slipped her mouth over him, sucking him into her mouth.

He groaned, pulling her head closer, holding it where he wanted. He thrust deeper into her throat.

Faith choked, the unfamiliar actions taking her by surprise. His firmness stretched her lips, bumping the roof of her mouth. The salty flavor spreading with each thrust. Faith swallowed. The action pulled him deeper. Her gasp took even more. She gagged.

He pulled slightly out and thrust in again. The firm feel of his hands in her hair, the salty musk coating her taste buds thrilled her. The tightness of her lips, the slight pain to take him in excited her.

Grasping his thighs, Faith gave herself up to his ministrations. She squirmed. Heat filled her sex, leaving her wanting. Her breasts hung heavy, her nipples hard and aching. She slid one hand down to squeeze her breast, titillating her nipple.

He groaned, pulling her face firmly against him. His coarse hairs tickling her nose. He groaned and pulsed inside her mouth.

Faith swallowed, unable to pull back. Hot, thick cream poured down her throat, filling her cheeks and slipping out her mouth to dribble down her chin. She shook, her sex empty and wanting. She sucked, eagerly seeking more. He pulsed, then pulled free of her mouth. Faith mewled. She wanted more.

"Fuck."

The stranger pushed her down, pulling at her clothes until they were scattered around her. Faith ached, hungry for something more. She spread her legs, shameless in her desire. Hoping this man could give her what she needed. Her core ached, throbbing and grasping at air. Faith dripped, her desire sliding down, rounding her buttocks.

"So pretty."

Faith squirmed. Callused fingers traced the petals of her sex, dipping in to tease her, sliding easily in her juices. "Please." Faith wasn't sure exactly what she was asking for, but the emptiness needed to be filled, the hunger teaming through her blood assuaged. The cock of the man before her looked made to do the job.

"You don't have to beg." He slid down, his face pressing against her privates. "Mmmmm."

"Oh God." The vibration of his mouth against her pussy making her shake. More, she wanted more. "Please." Faith grasped his hair, pushing his head against her. She tilted her hips, seeking something to ease her.

A warm tongue speared her, entering her, thrusting in and out. Faith pulled him closer, spreading her legs farther apart. "'s good." She couldn't have imagined this. His thick warm tongue felt wonderful dipping in and out of her. She burned.

His hands held her down, keeping her thighs spread. He nibbled, teeth scrapping her sensitive nub.

Faith jerked, the sensation exquisite. He chuckled. Faith shuddered. He grabbed her breasts, squeezing and plucking her nipples. He thrust his tongue in, slurping at the honey he coaxed from her. He pulled free and latched onto her clit, sucking and teasing her. He released a breast and pushed a long thick finger into her, growled and sucked hard.

Faith shattered. Her arms flailed latching onto his hair, arching against his lips, teeth and tongue. Oh god! She undulated against his mouth. His hot tongue the catalyst to driving her into ecstasy. He drew her orgasm out until Faith dropped her hips, trying to push him away.

"Not done." He swatted her arms away. He pulled back, grinned and lapped at her pussy. "Got to clean up."

Faith flushed and squirmed. His tongue spreading heat across her with each lick of his thick tongue. "Stop." She melted, loving the heat of his tongue eating her sex.

"Nope." He grinned against her.

Faith swallowed, his teeth, then his lips nibbled her. Between licks, he worked his way from her sheath up, going back to play. Faith jolted, sensitive everywhere he touched. He nibbled each lower lip. Faith giggled. He wasn't quiet, letting her know he was enjoying himself. Faith felt like a chew toy. He nibbled up, his teeth worrying her clit. The bit of sensitive flesh pulsed at his caress. Faith moaned, tilting up to give him better access. His fingers spread her, caressing her hood. She wiggled. It felt so good. The tip of his tongue made contact, teasing the bud. Suddenly he bit down. Faith squeaked. Then his lips sucked, his tongue flicking her. Faith screamed, legs wrapping around his head.

CHAPTER FOUR

Her legs squeezed his head. Crag pried them apart, sliding up her body and thrusting home while Faith fell apart. He needed the tight wet sheath around his cock. He sank in, plowing through her virgin flesh. Crag felt the bit of flesh and tore through it. Her gasp told him she was his. He jerked forward, his balls slapping against her ass, until nothing separated them.

"Mine."

Faith whimpered below him. Her nipples were hard and twisted, a deep raspberry red. They rubbed against his chest, exciting him more. He hadn't thought it possible.

Crag leaned down, latching onto a nipple and sucked in time with his thrusts. God she was so tight. Hot. Wet.

Faith's arms and legs came around him, holding on. Crag pounded into her, his balls slapping her ass with each thrust. His cock rubbed against her clit with each shift in. Crag slid a hand down, his fingers seeking. He rubbed her clit, grinding down each time he filled her. Her slick tight channel squeezed him, making his balls ache and his cock throb and lengthen. He'd never been so hard. He quickened, unable to stop. Her juices just enough lubrication to keep him from tearing her apart. He wanted to pound into her forever, his cock nestled in her tight silkiness.

Faith moaned. Her sheath pulsed, pulling his ejaculation from him. Each squeeze was answered by an echoing throb from him. Crag sprawled over Faith. It could only be Faith from her scent. She lay boneless beneath him. Her arms and legs slid down, splayed beneath him in the grass.

"Move. Heavy." Her arms made a feeble attempt to push him off before falling back against the ground.

Crag chuckled and shifted, groaning as he slid from her. He rolled to the side, slipping an arm under Faith's head and pulling her into his arms.

She groaned and snuggled close.

"Mine." The rumble of his dragon escaped with the word. His dragon confirmed Faith was his mate, as he'd thought. Not that he'd had any doubt.

"Not. Have to rescue..." Her words were slurred. One hand patted his side before sliding down to rest against his butt.

"Mine." Crag frowned, looking down. All he could see was her abundant fair hair.

"Nuh uh." With a sigh she fell asleep.

He glared, frustrated at her denial. When she woke, she would find out the truth. She was his. Made for him by the fates. She would have to find a way to except it.

Pulling her close, enjoying the silkiness of her skin next to his, he sighed. She was right where she belonged. Nothing would change that.

Thinking of her words, Crag wondered what she'd meant. Have to rescue. Who or what? The only person he could think of was the young woman missing from her village.

Could Faith have found a clue about her location? Or what happened to her?

Tempted to wake her, Crag sighed. Watching her sleep peacefully, he decided that it could wait. He'd have to ask Faith once she awoke. The woman had been missing for a while. Letting Faith sleep would not change what her fate.

Her breath blew warm across him. Her eyes fluttered, movement behind her lids signifying she was dreaming. Her legs entwined with his.

He hoped her dream was about him. He grinned, running his hand along her spine, loving her pressed against him. He was glad his brothers had turned back, appreciating this time alone with his mate. Once his family arrived, and they would, they just couldn't help themselves, he and Faith would be hard pressed to find alone time. He had no desire to share her, but he wanted his mate to become a dragon.

He could just imagine her dragon. In stature, Faith was littler than her sister. He'd bet anything she would also be a tiny dragon. What had he told Ari? A pocket dragon. Crag chuckled. She'd be a pale golden, like her hair. Adorable and feisty. And all his. He couldn't wait to begin their life together.

His heart raced, contentment spreading to his toes. He could see Faith, round with eggs. Glowing in gloriousness. His arms tightened, pulling her against him, cocooning her small body.

He would adore their hatchlings. He would protect them from anything, teaching them everything they would need to know.

He just had to change her.

Crag pulled her close and shut his eyes, his body wrapped around his mate's, enjoying the fact that in her sleep, she was embracing him back.

Dusk was approaching and with his mate safe beside him, he could finally sleep without a care. No animal would dare bother a dragon, sleeping or awake.

CHAPTER FIVE

Faith wiggled from his arms, mourning the loss of his warmth. Crawling backward, moving bit by bit to escape his embrace. He didn't wake, one arm sliding to rest on his chest, the other on the ground. Free from his limbs, she couldn't help but stare for a bit.

Heavily muscular, he was mouthwateringly fit. His six-pack led teasingly down toward his groin and his bulk showed he liked his food. His abdomen, obviously tight and in shape, but his waist carried just a bit of a love handle, proving he loved his food. Smothering a smile, Faith wanted to wake him and tease him, just a bit.

Despite knowing the foolishness of that desire, when she had to leave, she followed his glory trail south. The sight of his large, thick, flaccid penis dried her mouth. Moisture settling south, drenching her pussy. The ache in her abdomen, the racing of her heart, assured her that settling down and straddling him was an awesome idea. Just imagining him sliding into her shortened her breath.

Leaning forward, knowing it was pure foolishness, Faith licked him from his root to his tip. Pulling back, his cock rose following her mouth. Licking her lips, she suckled the tip. Her hips tilted, wanting to feel him inside. He tasted so good. Salty and manly.

Faith giggled. He moaned. She stilled. Flicking out her tongue, she licked him, sucking lightly. He grew, filling her mouth. Unable to resist, Faith bobbed down, taking as much of him as she could. Her fingers slid into action, one hand caressing his large sac and the other grasping him at the root, holding him up for her pleasure.

Nipples pebbling, juices running down her thighs, Faith suckled. She rubbed her nipples against his thigh, the sensations shooting through her belly to land in her throbbing clit.

The man growled, arching up. Ramming his cock down her throat.

Choking, Faith peeked up. His eyes were closed, his mouth open just a bit, drool on one side. She stifled her amusement. Still asleep. If he was still asleep, he would never know. Pulling back, Faith double checked. He was definitely asleep.

Crawling over him, Faith straddled him. Grasping his cock, she rubbed it against her aching clit. Biting her lips, she savored the feeling. He was hot, hard, and ready even in his sleep. Raising up, Faith guided him into her aching, juicy pussy. Sliding down slowly, she gasped. Wiggling, she fit him inside. His thickness and length stretching her until she was seating fully on him. Groaning quietly, trying to remember to be quiet, Faith rocked.

Her breath caught. The tinge of soreness compounded by his cock hair abrading her clit sent shivers up her spine. Faith tilted her head back, gasping at the sensations running through her body.

Her hands grabbed her boobs, tugging at her nipples. She needed more. Faith bounced, sliding up and down his hard length, luxuriating in the feelings. Sliding one hand down, she circled her clit, rubbing harder, bouncing harder on him. Groaning at the sensations bombarding her.

Her world shifted beneath her. A hand pulled her forward sending her off balance. A mouth latched onto her breast, suckling. Teeth scraping her nipple. A rough finger replaced her own, rubbing her clit. Faith bounced harder. Hands grasped her hips, forcing her to a pounding rhythm.

Faith screamed, pussy tightening on the cock filling her, trying to keep it in her body. The throbbing changed, warmth shooting into her depths, filling her. The pulsing of the cock inside her passage had her clenching down, wanting more. Wanting to keep him inside, massaging the parts of her body she never realized existed.

"Fuck, that's good." Arms crushed her, pulling her down across his body.

Her hips still humped his cock, still semi hard even after his explosion. Semen dripped down, lubricating their joining. Trembles chased across her body. Her clit pulsed. Faith loved the feel of his skin and hair and the slickness of their come rubbing against her pulsing pleasure point.

He grumbled, a hand sliding over her ass, fondling it. His hand cupped her cheek, moving her up and down. His fingers slid, one unerringly circling her star and sliding inside.

Faith froze. The sensations shocking her. She wasn't sure she liked it. She wiggled, trying to dislodge his finger.

A rumble vibrated his body. He slid further inside.

Faith trembled.

He bucked, penetrating her front and back. He wiggled his finger.

Faith clenched. Her juices helping him slip further into her.

He bucked, his hand on her ass, finger in her butt moving deeper and his dick growing.

Faith panted. Filled. With. Him.

He leaned forward, biting her breast, teasing her nipple, suckling her.

Faith whined, wiggled and exploded. She spread her legs wider taking all of his cock, rocking. His finger slid until his hand bottomed out. She rocked. She was so full, it drove her into a frenzy. Her clit ached. It was too much, but not enough. He had to have known.

He slid his other hand down, across her belly, kneading. Down to her pussy and rubbed her clit faster and faster.

Faith keened, her world whiting out, her pussy, her ass exploding in pleasure. She gasped as his finger slid out.

He grasped her hips, bouncing her on his dick.

Her ass felt empty, but her pussy full. Heat speared her, her passage filled and burning. The drag of his cock extending her pleasure. Faith cried out, unable to keep quiet.

The man grunted, pounding inside her. He rolled, tucking Faith beneath him, spreading her legs, gazing at their joining. His hungry gaze making her belly clench.

Her nipples tightened, twisting into deep red berries. Her chest flushed with color. The heat ran under her skin, pooling between her legs.

He raised her legs, hanging them from his elbows. He was on his knees, pulling her toward him with each bang inside her.

She knew she would be bruised. Faith smiled, abdomen clenching.

He howled, warmth shooting into her. His throbbing sent her spiraling.

Faith cried out, twisting and turning at the sensations exploding inside her.

He dropped forward, covering her body. Warmth spreading where his skin touched hers.

"Best dream ever." The mumble barely reached her ears, followed by a loud snore.

Her eyes widened, amusement forcing out a snort.

Warm and comfortable, surrounded by his strength, she relaxed, eyes drooping. The last thing she heard was his snore.

He must have slid off her during the night. He lay sprawled next to her, emanating heat. Not enough to keep her warm though. It was for the best, despite her shivering.

Her body tingled pleasantly, achy in bits, but satiation made her movements languid. She'd never dreamed a man could make her feel like that. She'd been wild and out of control. He made her forget herself.

She couldn't do that, though. No matter how much she wanted to. She couldn't abandon Hope. Forgetting herself would make her lose time. She wasn't too upset about yesterday. Her lips quirked. Well, she wasn't at all upset about yesterday. Everything about the man she'd met sent her body out of control. Whirling into dizzying heights of pleasure she'd never imagined existed.

She sighed in appreciation. She couldn't help but think about him, wishing he could stay with her, despite knowing she didn't have the luxury to let him distract her any longer. Her mind wandered back to last night, thinking of the pleasure she took from him. She hadn't planned on spending the night learning about passion. Falling asleep, only to wake wrapped in his arms, then foolishly repeating it all over again.

Her stomach growled, reminding her of how long it had been since her last meal.

She'd forgotten her snare. She hoped it was full.

Faith stood up. This time, she knew better than to stare at his body. Gathering her clothes, she tiptoed to the river. Glancing back, she smothered a sigh.

He didn't move, sprawled across the grass in abandon.

Sliding into the cold water, shivering, but this time not in excitement, Faith quickly washed. She grabbed her canteen and filled it. Her stomach growling, she dried with her shirt. It would be a little damp but better than everything sticking to her. Her jacket would keep her warm.

Slipping on her clothes, Faith headed to her snare. Spying it, relief washed over her. In it hung a rabbit. Thanking the god her father insisted on praying to, Faith quickly emptied it. Setting it up again, she headed to the shelter she'd set up earlier.

The warmth of a fire and the smell of roasting meat had her eyes drooping. Faith curled up and when the rabbit was done, ate her fill. She had a bit of time left before morning. Wrapping the leftovers and storing them in her satchel, she fell asleep. Warm, full, and satiated.

The rays of the rising sun woke her. Even if she couldn't see it. She always rose when the sun barely rose in the sky. Putting out the fire, making sure it wouldn't spread from unattended embers, Faith ensured she had all her belongings. There weren't many, but she needed them all to survive.

Crawling out of her shelter, she stood, stretching. Glancing back toward where she left the man snoring away, a smile tickled her lips. Standing still, she could still hear him. If only she could keep him. But she had a mission. Rescue her sister.

Shaking away her daydreams, Faith turned. She'd check her snare one more time. Empty or full, she needed it. Heading toward the river, she was ecstatic to see it was once again full. Quickly preparing the animal for travel, Faith wrapped up the snare, placing both in her satchel.

Checking her compass one more time, Faith took a last glance behind her, and headed out. The man would only slow her down. Most men wanted their own way, expecting the woman to listen. She couldn't afford to. Faith needed to gain on the creatures that had stolen her sister, screaming, away from her family.

Her compass kept her on the path she could only pray would lead to her sister.

CHAPTER SIX

Crag stretched; his body relaxed. The sun was peeking over the tree tops, the brightness of the rays teasing him into wakefulness.

A slight breeze cooled his warm skin. He tended to run hotter than his brothers. His dam insisted it was because he was always eating. His stomach rumbled, reminding him it was time for breakfast.

He grabbed his morning wood and gave it a stroke. His mate could take care of this, he didn't have to. He thickened, imaging her tongue tracing his dick. His dreams from the night before filled his mind. Making love to his mate, rather, her making love to him, straddling his body with abandon. If he didn't know better, he'd swear it wasn't a dream. Crag rolled over, turning toward his mate. Reaching out, he encountered emptiness.

He jumped up, looking all around. Faith was not next to him where he expected, not even anywhere in sight.

Maybe she was answering a call of nature. Looking around, he nodded, it made sense. Ari said his mate was innately shy about him being near when she did so. Crag snorted. Humans could be odd. He cocked his head, listening. His dragon hearing greater than a human. He frowned. No Faith. Glancing around where they slept, his lips tightened. Her gear was gone.

"Damn it."

It appeared she snuck off. He tended to be a heavy sleeper. Since he didn't worry about predators, he had no problem sleeping. In this case, exhaustion and satisfaction had sent him into a deep sleep. What kind of a mate was he? He should be attuned to Faith, be able to anticipate her every need. He harrumphed, taking in the Faithless area around him.

She couldn't be too far away. All he had to do was catch up. He didn't know how long she'd been gone. The sex had wiped him out. It had just been getting dark and her warmth and his full belly lulled him to sleep. Having his mate in his arms filled him with contentment. He chuckled. Too much so, since he had slept through her rising and leaving.

Crag looked around and frowned. He really didn't know when she left. She was out of hearing range. He stood up and dove into the water, bringing out his dragon. Fish sounded like a fine idea for breakfast. Then he'd go hunt down Faith.

The water sloughed off the grit, allowing his scales to gleam. The sun sent rays of light shining down on his scales, sending flickers of light into the water, attracting the curious fish. It made it easy to fill his mouth. The scales and bones crunched in his teeth. The slick feel of their flesh slid down his throat. He swallowed, savoring their flavor.

Flinging his head up, water arced, spraying rainbows across the river. Crag filled his lungs with the crisp air and rose, sending water and fish scurrying back with the power of his wings.

Crag shot up, above the trees. Spinning in effervescent joy. The currents of air eased his flight, the wind circling and drying his scales. He loved flying. His human body seemed slow and inefficient.

He smirked, thinking of the night before. It did have some advantages though. Just thinking of the silkiness of Faith's skin sent heat straight to his groin.

Not the best thing to happen in dragon form. It left him all too vulnerable if he flew too low to the treetops.

Crag spun with a grin and a final flourish, steadying out to glance out over the clearing. Dew still decorated the grass. He frowned, flying closer. Not even a hint of footsteps was evident. He wondered when Faith actually left. He skimmed the edge of the river. No footsteps could be seen there either. He shifted, landing on the balls of his feet.

She couldn't have left last night. Could she? Crag snorted. It was possible. His heart sped up thinking of the dangers she could face on her own. No one would bother him except another dragon. The only ones he knew were his siblings. There could be more dragons, he supposed. Mankind had made the world dangerous before practically eliminating themselves. He imagined most dragons had gone into hiding much like his clan. Thinking of Faith, Crag was glad the human race hadn't totally died out.

Searching the ground proving futile, Crag rose, grabbing his satchel, shifting and flying just above the trees. He would just have to find her. She was his after all, even if she didn't know it yet. He frowned. Even if she denied it. Crag circled the trees, looking for any sign of a path. Remembering spying something in the trees while flying yesterday, he headed that way.

Landing, he shifted again. Faith's spicy aroma lingered on the air. Now, he wondered whether her lingering scent was from yesterday or today. Crag ran his hands through his hair. Damn it, how come he didn't hear her leave? The sun overhead proved to him he slept later than he normally did. Disgusted with himself, he cursed. How could he protect his mate if she slipped away from him so easily? He would have to change his habits.

Sniffing, Crag closed his eyes, following the only one of his senses that could tell him where she went. He shuffled forward, nose in the air. He tripped, cursing and fell forward, landing face first in a large pine tree. Crag growled, struggling to get out. The branches swayed, shifting. Crag fell forward, sprawling out. The branches springing back into place.

Rolling over, Crag spied the remains of a fire. The earth blanketing it, still warm. Faith's scent permeating the area. So, this is where she'd run off to. Moving further under the shelter of the pine, he saw the impression of her body in the bed of needles on the ground. The air noticeably warmer beneath the tree.

Crag couldn't help but be impressed. Of course, if she had stayed with him all night she would have been plenty warm. The faint smell of blood told him she'd had a meal also.

He shook his head. He really had been out of it. He needed to sharpen his skills. He essentially left his mate unguarded last night. His own satisfaction taking precedence over all else. His dam would be sorely disappointed in him. Nostrils flaring, Crag wondered if he deserved a mate.

Look how easily she'd escaped his detection. Slipping out from under his nose. He backed out of her shelter, standing up. Finding her direction once again, Crag kept his eyes open this time, moving after her. Deserved or not, Faith was his. His to protect and love.

Her family needed her safe, as did he. Faith obviously had a destination in mind. If he returned her home, he wondered if she would just leave again.

Chuckling, Crag had a feeling she would.

Crag decided to follow on foot. Faith couldn't be too far ahead of him. Not to mention his stride was larger than hers. He shifted. Thinking of her skittishness of nudity, he slid on a pair of pants. It should be easy to catch up to her.

The path through the forest showed him it wasn't so. Afternoon had changed to evening and he still hadn't come across Faith. Her unique scent assured him he hadn't passed her. His size made passage hard. It was slowing him down more than he'd expected. But he was too close. He didn't want to find her as a dragon and scare her. Her sister had stabbed his brother when he'd taken her as a dragon. He could only imagine Faith's reaction. She had a knife, he'd seen it.

His stomach growled. Checking to make sure he still followed Faith's enticing aroma, he continued on. She'd have to stop for the night. He would just keep going until he found her. He frowned. This was taking longer to find her than he thought.

Backtracking, Crag found a spot where he could shift and fly out. Branches dragged at his wings, catching at his legs as he burst from the trees into the sky. Irritated, glancing down, he tried to locate Faith. Shaking his head, he flew higher. He didn't want her to see him, to be afraid of him. Hearing a scream, Crag paused. Circling where the sound came from, he listened carefully. It could have been a cougar, but he wasn't sure.

Peering down into the dense foliage, he shook his head. Nothing. His stomach twisted. He'd been following the river, far enough away that he wasn't sure Faith knew the river was still there. Heading toward the sound of the water, Crag decided to check. Perhaps she heard it and decided following it would speed her travels. He should have asked her where she was going instead of falling on her like a starving man.

Faith smelled faintly of dragon so she should be safe enough from predators. Once he'd fully claimed her, turned her, she'd never be vulnerable again.

Logically he knew that he would eventually have to tell her. But Faith seemed a little more intense than her sister. Somehow, Crag was pretty sure that if he changed Faith without telling her, he would regret it the rest of his life.

Already he could see that though Faith was younger than her sister she was not near as playful.

That suited him to a T. He prided himself on his level head. A frivolous girl would not do for him. Rog and Hark, he could see falling for some silly little thing. Faith was the perfect girl for him. A woman with a single-minded determination. For what, he hadn't quite figured out. He'd stick to her until she knew she couldn't live without him.

He'd help her achieve her goal.

His stomach growled, again, insistent on being fed. Up ahead, Crag spotted a herd of cattle. He grinned. His favorite, easy to catch and tasty to eat. A quick snack while he continued his search.

Pumping his wings, he increased his speed. Close enough for the cattle to get restless, sensing a predator near, he swooped down. Talons ripping through the hide, he clasped an animal in his grasp, flying away before the group could stampede.

Dropping it to the ground, he landed next to it. A few quick bites and it was gone. The warm taste of blood and the satisfying crunch of bone only teased the hunger. He would need more. Rising, his wings extended, Crag heaved into the sky. This time he'd catch two and then head back, continuing his search for Faith.

His shadow falling on the animals below, a distressed lowing met his ears. They were restless, missing the one member. Hooves stamping, crying to each other, they shifted below.

Narrowing his eyes, Crag scanned the herd. Finding two on the outskirts, he made his move. Swooping low, scattering them away from his targets, he successfully grabbed them and rose, a cow in each claw.

They struggled, lowing in distress.

He supposed to an animal that never left the ground, it was a scary experience. Landing, he quickly snapped their necks, dropping them to the ground.

Wolfing them down, Crag enjoyed the crunch that helped keep his teeth sharp. Finished, he burped, a small cloud of smoke rising from his nostrils. He needed to continue hunting his mate.

He stood, shaking his head and finishing with his tail, stretching out each joint.

Faith. He ached to be with her again. His hard body pressed against her softer one. He wanted her, needed her. Fate sent her to him, and he would keep her.

Even though she'd left him during the night. Even if she didn't say goodbye. Even though she'd alluded him all day. Groaning, Crag realized that she might not know he was searching for her. He smacked his head. He had never, not once called out for her.

Belly full, cracking his jaw, letting out just a bit of a roar, he prepared to fly.

Shadows swooped overhead, blocking the sun momentarily.

Crag braced himself and grumbled.

Two bodies dived at him. Landing too close on either side.

He stretched his wings, shoving them away. "Give a dragon some room."

Chuckles met his action and words.

"So, where's this mate?" Figures Rog would be the first to talk.

"Yeah, I don't see her." Hark always had to get a word in also.

"Did you lose her?"

"Or did she run away?"

"You're both a pain in the ass. What are you doing here?" He swung his tail, pushing away his brothers. Not that it did any good. He snarled, baring his long incisors.

They just laughed. Aggravating. His parents should have stopped with him. Or at least stamped on the other eggs. Those two eggs in particular. Ari was fine. His sisters were fine. But these two? Not fine.

"Where is she?" Rog asked again. Like he hadn't heard him the first time.

"Did you tell her? That you're a dragon?" Hark cocked his head, eyes full of mischief.

"She's walking and no, I didn't." Crag bit out the answer.

"You just left her? Alone, walking in the woods?" Rog shook his head, giving a huge theatrical sigh. "Really, poor thing. Abandoned by her mate, just to fill his stomach."

"That is why you left? To eat? You were hungry again?" Hark tried to hide his smirk, shaking his head.

Crag ground his teeth. My dam wouldn't be happy if I killed them. My dam wouldn't be happy if I killed them. He would just have to keep repeating it. Then again, he was pretty sure his sire would understand. He grunted, aggravated. His dam wouldn't though. His blood rose, heating the fire in his gut. Fire that would be absolutely useless against his brothers.

It would feel good though.

"If she's feeling neglected, maybe we should offer our services? We could guide her home. Right, Hark?"

"Yes, we could do that." Hark nodded in agreement with Rog.

"She's not neglected. She left me." Crag burst out, teeth grinding. "She's perfectly fine. As soon as I catch her, you'll see." Groaning, he dropped his head. Ignoring the howling laughter from his brothers. Damn it.

He'd never hear the end of it.

"She. Left. You." Rog rolled, stirring the dirt in the air.

Ass.

"Shut up." The hell with it. He shot a burst of flame at his brother. It settled the gurgling in his gut.

Rog's yelp was satisfying, even though Crag knew he wasn't hurt. Surprised, yes, but unfortunately not hurt. Dragon fire couldn't hurt another fire dragon. More's the pity.

Hark's snickering set his scales on edge.

Crag swung his tail, hitting him over the head with his knot. He was born a war dragon. Similar to his brothers but, his tail ended in a war knot, sharp protrusions that could reign down pain on his enemies.

That shut him up. Crag couldn't help but smirk. He hadn't hit him hard enough to hurt him. He knew. He'd had plenty of practice smacking his siblings to ensure he didn't leave marks. Or kill them.

"Stop that!" Hark scuttled away. Turning to face him, but far enough away from his tail.

Crag rolled his eyes. "Fine. You two, knock it off." He shuffled, sighing. "I woke up and she was gone. I followed her most of the day, but I needed to feed. I'll catch up to her."

"So where is she going? Why did she leave?" Rog walked closer, tail dragging behind him.

"I'm going to get something to eat." Hark muttered, shaking his head and flew into the air, his wings stirring the dirt toward them.

Crag coughed, scowling at his brother, watching him fly away.

"Grab me one!" Rog hollered after him.

Hark nodded, wings pumping, heading in the direction Crag had found the cattle.

"Why are you two here?"

Rog shrugged. "We figured we'd help. And the humans are crowded too close together."

"Any problems with the grandmother?"

"No, not really."

"She knows what we are."

"They all do now. At least Hope's family does." Rog shook his head, snorting.

"What happened?" Crag took a deep breath. This might not be bad. Maybe. Hopefully.

"Hope. What else?" His snicker didn't bode well.

"What did she do?" His gut ached. He needed to release more flame, or at least a bit of smoke. Dragons couldn't get ulcers. He was almost sure.

"She took her grandmother out to the barn and changed in front of her. Got beat by a broom from dear old grandma. Thought Hope had been eaten. Of course, the rest of the family came running with all the screaming."

"So, they know."

"Oh yeah, they know."

Both dragons stared at each other. This was what happened when Crag left his brothers on their own. Chaos. He growled, smoke releasing. The pressure in his gut eased.

"So, have they tried to kill you?" Crag would hate to terminate Faith's family but he would, if he had to.

"No. Once Faith is found, it looks like they are moving into the valley below your caverns."

"Fuck." Crag gritted his teeth, a low roar escaping his throat. "Even the grandmother?"

"Oh, yes." Rog snickered. "It was funny."

"I don't even want to know." He didn't. As long as no one tried to kill his brothers despite how aggravating they were, they could live.

A cow slammed down from the sky, landing with a thud. Followed by a second, and a third. Crag jumped, startled.

Hark's laughter trumpeted from the sky.

Rog grabbed one, crunching and munching.

Hark landed, pulling one beast toward himself. He pushed the third at Crag. "Just in case you're still hungry. Plus, you could take some back to your mate."

Crag's skin flushed. Lucky his scales hid it. He pulled the steer toward him, ashamed that he had not thought to provide for his mate. He swallowed, his words low. "Thank you."

What kind of a mate was he? He didn't notice when she left him. He hadn't even thought to provide a meal for her. She was thin, too thin. Something that should have triggered his protective instincts. Instead all he wanted was to sink his cock in her.

Damn it. When he found her, he would do better.

"I need to get back to Faith." He grabbed the steer with one claw. "I'll see you two later." Hopefully whatever mischief they decided on would be far away from his mate.

He lifted off, their nods the only reassurance he got. He wasn't going to count on them staying away. They never did.

Soaring above them, circling, Crag continued searching. There was no evidence of Faith along the river. She must still be hidden in the trees. He could do nothing about his brothers and it was useless to worry. They would do what they wanted.

Crag's thoughts turned back to his mate, his claws tightening on the prey in his talons. The thought of her body in the light of the fire, flames flickering off her skin had him once again aching. Flying with a hard on was a pain in the ass. Growling, disgusted with himself, he turned his thoughts to something, anything, else.

He would try to put his dragon's desires away and listen to her. Be a better mate to Faith. After all, what kind of mate didn't even feed her? He would pay attention to her body language. His blood rose, thinking of her body. Damn it. If he could keep from thinking with his aching cock.

CHAPTER SEVEN

Faith slowed down. She ignored the fact that she was alone. Her choice. She'd left. She refused to acknowledge the hope that the man would come after her. He hadn't. She hadn't been going that fast.

Looking up, she cried out, quickly muffling her cry with her hands. Above her circled a dragon. She hid beside a tree trunk, hoping she blended in. Maybe if she was captured, she'd find Hope sooner. But what if it took her somewhere else?

She couldn't chance it. Wouldn't she look like an idiot if she ran after it, yelling and waving her arms?

Looking up, Faith gasped. Two more dragons were headed her way. She had to be closer to locating her sister.

Her lips firmed. She would find her sister. Rescue her. Defeat the dragons. Or at least run away from them. Then Faith would set off on her adventure.

Even if her niggling thoughts told her this was one wild adventure, she ignored them. Rescuing her sister wasn't an adventure. It was her sister. Hope would do the same for her. Even if she wanted to run far and fast from her family, it wasn't them. It was the sameness, day after day of doing the same thing, seeing the same people.

The crunch of broken branches beneath her feet kept her stepping carefully. She didn't need to sprain her ankle or fall due to moving hastily. Glancing up at the sky, Faith checked to see if any more dragons were there.

Between the branches, glimpses of the mythological creatures fueled her determination. The sound of the water off to her side got louder. They looked to be following the water. Better yet, they were heading in the direction the other one had gone.

Faith stalled to a halt. What if she stumbled onto the dragon's lair? Would she be able to find Hope? She refused to wonder if Hope was alive. She was. She had to be. Hope was smart. She knew how to use any number of weapons. Hope rarely left the house without a knife and a bow and arrow at the minimum.

Maybe she had managed to escape. If Hope headed home, Faith should run into her. Hope could survive in the wilderness. She'd find her way home. But just in case, Faith was ready and willing to save her.

Tramping through the wilderness, Faith sighed. The dragon was no longer in sight. But she kept going. Nothing and no one could hold her back. Not that she had anyone to do so.

Her mind wandered. She should have asked his name. Instead, all she had was the remembrance of his firm body against hers, in hers. Her breath quickened, a shiver delicately rode her spine from neck to tailbone. His large calloused hands were perfect. Rough enough, strong enough to move her how he wanted.

The afternoon light cast larger shadows on the forest floor. Faith munched on a handful of trail mix. The cool air felt good against her skin. A small sheen of perspiration coated her body. She slowed. She'd never catch up to the flying creature. She needed to pace herself. Maybe... maybe she would make better time if she followed the river, running along the bank. With no trees in her way, and hopefully ground without roots grabbing out to trip her, she'd gain more speed.

Draining the last of her canteen, Faith sighed. She needed to fill it. Turning, she headed in the direction of the water. The river it was.

Hopefully no dangerous animals were around. She could always dart away to the cover of the trees. The sound of the river increased. Peering from between the trees, Faith checked out the river bank.

Good. Clear. Faith left the trees, hurrying to the river. She smiled. The area was beautiful. Empty of any predators. Faith gazed longingly at the water. Crouching down, she dipped her hand in it. Goosebumps ran up her arm, but it felt good.

She submerged her canteen, filling it. Glancing around, Faith stood. No one and nothing were around. Capping her water, making sure it wouldn't leak, she dropped it to the ground.

She swiveled her head, looking around one more time. Clear of anything. No predators of any type. A smile graced her lips. She dropped her bag to the ground. Faith stripped, removing first her shirt then her pants, taking off every bit of clothing.

She grinned, spreading her arms and spinning in the warm of the afternoon light. Free. Her spirit had never felt so light before. Even knowing Hope was in danger couldn't dampen her joy.

Dizzy, giggling, Faith stopped. The earth dipped then steadied. Running forward Faith splashed into the river. Taking a deep breath, she dove beneath the surface, arms slicing through the water. She submerged, summersaulting, the water like silk against her skin. Goosebumps slithered down her spine. The sweat washed away, leaving her refreshed. Rising to the surface, the afternoon sun reflected off the water, shimmering, blinding her, her arms arcing through the air.

Faith screamed. Something soft, foreign grasped her, pulling her out of the water. Sharp nails threatened to slice her in pieces. Water streaming down her face from her hair blocking her vision. Whatever it was, was monstrous! The claws clasped her loosely, dragging her into the air.

Frantically wiping her eyes clear, Faith gasped. A dragon!

She struggled, slipping. If she could only get free! It hovered over the water, eying her curiously. She could land in the river safely. Wiggling, she tried to pry from its grip. She slipped. It tightened its grip. Not enough to hurt. But it wouldn't let her go.

Faith pulled back, shaking, pulling, pushing, anything to get loose.

Its head twisted putting its face near hers. A large eye stared at her, its mouth too close.

Oh God! Its teeth were huge! The tremble started with her teeth, her body shaking in fear. Her gut tightened, her body shrinking.

"No!" She would be damned if she died a cowering mess. The monster would have to earn this meal. Screwing up her courage, Faith lunged, screaming in defiance, arms aimed at its snout.

She connected, beating as hard as she could. Rational thought escaped her.

Looking into its eyes she swore she saw surprise then amusement.

Growling, she swung, putting all her strength behind her flailing fists. It didn't matter if she hit it every time. She wanted to do as much damage as she could.

The dragon's claws released her, sending her plunging through the air.

"Ahhh!" Pain stung her body. Her back slapping the water with painful intensity. Water engulfed her, suffocating her. She sank, touching the bottom, then pushing up toward the dull light she could only hope was the sun. Her lungs ached, painfully needing air. Almost there.

Her face broke the water. She drew in a deep breath, and a loud rumble reached her ears. Shaking her head, clearing her eyes, Faith looked up. Eyes widening, she started scrambling away. Two dragons fought above her. If they hadn't stolen her sister and tried to steal her, she might, just might, enjoy the wonder of seeing them close up. They gracefully flew through the sky, diving and growling, shooting flames at each other.

Faith squeaked and dropped underwater, the flame heating the air near her head. Shaking her head at her own foolishness, she dove deeper, swimming away from the fighting pair.

Coming up for air, she felt the bottom beneath her feet. Glancing back, seeing the fight continuing, Faith backed slowly out of the water, keeping her eye on the pair. If she was quick enough, hopefully she could escape into the trees. Their size should prevent them from following her. Her body prickled, shivering from the change in temperature.

Heart racing, she whirled, ran, stopping with a sudden jerk, hitting what felt like a wall. Bouncing back, falling from the force to the ground. Another one! This one eyed her curiously, head cocked. And he was sitting on her clothes. This dragon didn't seem aggressive. But Faith worried it was a matter of time before he decided to eat her or not.

He roared and Faith curled up into a ball. The heat from his breath assaulting her nose. Her gorge rose. Swallowing to keep from vomiting, she shook her head, scuttling back toward the water.

The sudden silence penetrated her senses. Freezing, stomach dropping, Faith gazed behind her. The dragons circled her, giving her no way out. The black one, the one with the hint of green to his scales narrowed his eyes, growling at the one next to him. The one he'd been fighting. He loomed over her.

If she didn't know better, she'd swear he was protecting her. Glancing at his large belly, she inched away. Nope, he was just guarding his food. His gut told the story. This dragon didn't share his food. Faith stared, she swore this dragon was the one she had seen earlier a few days ago on the bank of the river. She squinted peering closer. Yes, yes it had to be the same dragon. She muffled her mouth with a shaking hand, stifling a nervous giggle. This was definitely the beast she saw humping the riverbank.

She took a step closer to him. Suddenly she was dragged closer, its tail wrapping around her waist pulling her to his side. Faith squealed. Her naked body smashed against the scales. They were much softer than they looked. She couldn't even touch them though, her arms tight against her own body as he held her there, not even looking at her. A shiver ran up her spine. She had absolutely no idea what was going to happen to her. It was obvious she had no power and was just a pawn. All she could do was wait and make a run for it when she had a chance.

CHAPTER EIGHT

His damn brothers!

Crag tightened his tail around Faith, pulling her against him. Her silky skin sending a shiver through his large body. His body ached at the contact.

Ignoring the sparking from her touch, Crag roared, threatening his brothers. Faith wiggled against him, trying to get away. He growled, flattening her against his side.

His brothers laughed, though the way Faith cowered against him, she didn't realize it. He lunged at Hark, keeping Faith tight against him. She squealed, the scent of her fear meeting his nose.

What do you think you are doing? Can't you tell how scared she is?

We're just trying to help. Right Rog?

Sure, we don't mean any harm. Why don't you change? Or doesn't she know that you're a man too? Hark snickered.

Crag growled, baring his teeth. *You know I haven't told her.*

You know, the longer you wait, the harder it will be. Rog tried to look innocent, but the glint in his eye gave him away.

Just go away. Crag gnashed his teeth. His dam would not forgive bite marks on his brother's neck. He was tempted to try all the same.

Sure, sure. Come on, Hark. Let's go. We can tell when we're not wanted.

With a bit of splashing around, a few growls and a belch of flame towards his head, his brothers finally departed.

Crag turned his head and looked at Faith. Her face was pale. She shivered in place against him. She wasn't even struggling anymore. Crag loosened his tail. She stood still letting his coiled tail unwrap from around her body. He swallowed. She tempted him even in his natural body. Luckily, she couldn't see the effect she was having on him.

Until he made known to her that he could shift between forms, he didn't think it was a good idea to show her. He wasn't a saint though, no dragon he knew was.

He flicked his tail up, running the tip down her body, as flexible as another hand. He rounded her curves, feeling the weight of her breasts. Lightly squeezing them, the tip teasing her nipples.

Her heartbeat sped up, a flush rising along her body. Her breath caught, but Crag didn't think it was in fear.

His nostrils flared. He flicked his tongue out, wanting to taste.

Faith's eyes widened, and she scrambled backwards. She landed against the thickest part of his tail where it connected to his body. She looked wildly around. Her scent hadn't changed though.

He wielded his tail slighting the tip around her ankle and tugging.

Off-balance, she widened her stance trying to stay upright.

Crag tightened his tail, keeping one ankle in his grasp. His head moved closer to her, sniffing her. Running his snout against her body, his tongue flicking, tasting her nipples, sliding down her belly. He took a deep breath, her scent making his eyes roll back in delight.

He couldn't resist. His tongue shot out licking the plump petals.

Her muffled gasp only encouraged him. Her legs widened infinitesimally.

It was good enough for him. Snuffling he wedged between her legs as much as he could. His tongue played, tasting her sex. Flickering, teasing and dipping into the sweetest nectar he'd ever tasted.

He wanted more. He wanted to sink between her legs and never come up.

Her soft hands were on his head tugging at his ears. He winced. She was pulling harsher than he expected. Crag pulled back, looking up at her. Her fist popped against his nose.

Startled, he moved back further. Her face was flushed, her cheeks ruddy. The glint in her eyes had him blinking. She looked furious. He nuzzled her crotch, sniffing. She was still wet. A flick of his tongue to taste her assured him of her arousal.

Her screech made him wince. He cocked his head looking at her. He didn't quite understand. She looked angry, but she was enjoying what he was doing. Maybe she was cold in the water. He backed up toward the riverbank. Ensuring she moved with him without stumbling.

Once on dry land, the grass tickling the underside of his belly, Crag held her against him. There, now she wouldn't have to worry about slipping. The sun warm on his back, he nuzzled once again between her legs.

She slid down, her bottom landing on the grass, arms waving in the air.

This was even better. He wouldn't have to worry about her falling or drowning in the water. He shuffled around, facing more towards her. His front feet grabbed her ankles, spreading them. He made sure to retract his talons. Crag didn't want to cause her pain by accidentally scratching her.

He dove in, drawn by her scent. His tongue separated her petals, flicking over the jewel peeking from between her legs.

Faith squealed. Her hands once again grabbing his ears.

He ignored her tugging. Her sweetness assuring him that she was enjoying his attentions. His tongue slid into her damp passage. His erection lengthened, enough so that he could no longer sit flat against the grass. His haunches raised giving room to the steel hardness between his legs.

"Stop!"

There was too much nectar to make him believe she wanted him to really stop. Her wiggling bottom was in direct contrast to her words.

He breathed deep, wanting to come closer to her. Screw it, he needed her. He would deal with the fallout later. Faith was his and he wasn't letting her go.

A particularly hard slap had his ears ringing.

"I said stop." Faith growled. "Here I am talking to what has to be the dumbest animal in the world. It can't understand me."

Crag growled. He wasn't stupid. Horny, yes. He could pound nails with how hard he was. Seeing Faith sprawled on the ground, her torso held up by her elbows as she glared at him just made him hot. His feet still held her legs spread open showing him her pink bits glistening from her juices.

She tugged her ankles trying to free herself.

Crag lengthened his talons, careful not to scratch Faith. He dug them into the dirt giving her very little room to move.

Faith bucked, bringing her closer to his mouth before landing back on the ground.

"Do that again." His voice gravelly, unused to speaking out loud.

"Ahh! You spoke!" She wiggled, trying to get away from him. "I must be going crazy!"

"Do that again." Crag held her, not letting her get away.

She growled. It was so cute. It just turned him on more. He admitted to himself, he might be just a bit perverse. They were a good match.

She tugged her ankles again trying to get free. Her hands pushed against his face.

He slid his tongue out licking her fingers.

Faith squealed letting go. She twisted bucking again.

He was ready for her this time. His tongue slid the length of her bottom, dipping in to her honey hole before she again hit the ground.

He knew there would be hell to pay. That wasn't going to stop him. Diving forward, sliding up her body, he shifted, changing into his human form.

He groaned, his cock sliding home, wincing at the pain of her nails in his back.

CHAPTER NINE

What the hell!

Faith gripped the man above her, fingers digging into his back. His cock deep in her body, filling every empty space. She shivered, looking in his face, and gasping. No way!

Just a moment ago she was being eaten out by a dragon. Trying to get away. Her mind telling her that it was oh, so wrong, but her body begging for more.

Now, a man pinned her down. Not just any man, but the stranger she left behind.

"What are you?" Her breath caught.

He grunted. His body rocking into hers. A wild look in his eye, speech apparently beyond him.

His mouth dipped down. His tongue teasing her nipple, before sucking the tip of her breast in his mouth. The rhythmic suction set her squirming. Her juices lubricating his breaching of her body.

Her lungs seized, her breath caught. His slickness sliding in and out, pleasure so intense, her eyes rolled to the back of her head. Her senses centering on their connection, her abdomen clenching in delight. This couldn't be real. This man, the man she thought she left behind; the stranger who made her want to stay. He couldn't be a dragon. He couldn't. Could he?

She must be losing her mind. She was hallucinating, she had to be. How on earth was she supposed to accept that one minute he was a monster and the next a man?

"Faith." He groaned her name.

It only emphasized the fact that she didn't know his.

"Who the hell are you?" She tried to sound angry, but she came off breathless even to her own ears.

His groans and the slap of flesh against flesh echoed in the clearing. Her pulse pounded; her body thrilled to be touching his. Had she somehow known that the monster was this man? Her mind rebelled. She shook her head but couldn't help mewling as his lips slid down her throat.

Her mind succumbed to the demands of her body. Her shallow pants, her racing pulse, and an utter thrill racing through her bloodstream from the thick shaft sliding in and out of her helped to wipe her mind clean.

Faith curled her legs around his hips, keeping him as close to her as she could. Her hands scored down his back leaving her mark in blood.

It didn't matter what his name was. Only his touch did. Her pussy clenched, aching around his cock. Pulling him deep inside, her breath shortened. Goosebumps raced along her skin. Her nipples tight and aching.

Mindless her body cried for more.

"Who are you?" She could barely get the words out.

"I'm your mate."

His answer reverberated through her soul. But that still did not answer her question. "And whose name should I cry out when I come?"

The rumble in his chest sent tremors of ecstasy through her. His deep laughter spilled around them. "Crag. My name is Crag."

He thrust deep into her body, slamming her against the ground, again and again. He pulsed inside her, growing impossibly larger, shattering her soul.

A soundless scream erupted from her throat. Heat filled her, spilling out between them with each rhythmic movement of their frantic bodies.

His thrusts slowed. His breathing heavy in the air. Each deep breath pressed his chest against her sensitive nipples. His weight settled on hers. Her aching breasts finding relief. She knew his name.

Her arms dropped to the ground. Sated to her toes, legs still wrapped around Crag's waist, Faith exhaled. Crag was large enough to cover every inch of her. His warmth seeped into her limbs. Her breathing evened out. Thought once again trickled into her brain.

Her breath caught. Unwrapping her legs, she shoved him away. Or she tried.

"What?" He licked her neck, sending a shiver down her spine.

"Get off me. What is wrong with you?" She shoved at him again. "What are you?"

What she'd seen was impossible. Pushing him only pressed his chest back and his hips drilled deeper, sending a tickle of pleasure down her spine. Her eyes rolled back. His slightest move sent fire through her veins.

Faith gathered her courage. Sucking in a breath, she couldn't succumb to whatever magic this was. She couldn't. She'd never seen or heard anything like this.

Men becoming monsters.

Monsters becoming men. Her brain rebelled at what her eyes had clearly seen.

"Dragon. I saw you change from a dragon." Her arms pushed futilely against him.

He grinned. His length slid from her body. He slid to her side gathering her close, his arms wrapping around her. "So? What is wrong with that? I'm a man right now."

"Everything. It can't be real." Faith dropped her head against his chest.

"Sure, it can. It is *my* reality."

Faith burrowed deeper into his chest. Her hands gripping his waist. Her brain hurt. The evidence in front of her, in her arms, was hard to deny. But that was the hard part. If she accepted that he could indeed become a dragon, she wondered what he'd done with her sister.

"Then where is my sister?" Faith feared the answer. A chill slipped through her body, freezing her veins. She feared the worst. There could only be so many dragons. It would be too big of a coincidence for there to be more.

"Hope? She is with her mate." His arms tightened around her pulling her snugly against him.

"I don't understand. I saw Hope stolen. I heard her screaming. I need to know she's okay." Faith poked at him, digging into his chest. Her ears felt aflame. Her chest tight. Her emotions swung from one extreme to the other. "I need to see my sister."

Hope's screams echoed in her memory. She should be scared of him, but the lassitude of her limbs, the sleepiness and pleasure he had given her, failed to make that connection.

"I need to know she's okay." A niggling jealousy entered her mind. Could he have done this to Hope? She really hoped not. Just the thought churned her stomach.

Faith flopped onto her back, his arm still cushioning her head. Oh, what was wrong with her? She couldn't, wouldn't believe that he'd shared this with Hope.

His arm pulled her back against him. His lips touched her hair in a tender kiss. His other arm coming around her to rub her back.

"I swear to you that she's okay. More than okay. She's with my brother."

All the tension drained from her body. Faith could hear the truth in his voice. She worried she wanted to believe him so bad that she was blinding herself to the truth. No matter what she hoped, she needed to know.

"Promise? She's alive? Not eaten?"

"I promise. Alive and well. Joyful, even." His hand traced her curves, brushing against her sensitive flesh.

Faith lay next to him. Her heart racing, lungs ready to bust. Taking a deep breath, worrying if she really should trust him, she exhaled. She believed him. At least, she'd try. Perhaps she was being naïve. But he'd protected her from the other dragons. He knew Hope. Or he said he did. The touch of his hands sent goosebumps skittering across her skin.

He snickered next to her. "I can't promise she wasn't eaten though. Ari can't keep his hands and mouth off her."

She rolled her eyes, relaxing a little bit more. Dragon or not, his humor was as bad as the men she knew at home. She ignored his meandering fingers, wanting more information.

"Ari is your brother?"

"Yes."

"And he's the one I saw snatch Hope?"

"You saw that, huh?"

Faith nodded her head. She kept picturing it, scared that was the last time she'd see her sister. "I thought I'd never see her again." She swallowed. If she found out he was lying to her, she'd gut him.

His hand rubbed her back, pulling her against his chest, offering comfort.

"We could see them in just a couple of hours if you'd like. We could fly."

Her eyes widened. "What? Like on dragon back?"

Crag snorted. "No. Yes. No," he cleared his throat, "like dragons."

Faith craned her head up, trying to look into his eyes. "In case you didn't know it, I'm not a dragon."

"Would you like to be?"

What? She couldn't have heard him right.

"Hope loves being a dragon." His voice was tentative. The words seeming to come reluctantly from his mouth.

"What?" She couldn't have heard that correctly. "I know my sister. She isn't a dragon. No more than I am."

"Yes, she is. Ari changed her." Crag nuzzled her neck, sending shivers down her spine. "He's her mate, like you're mine."

Faith stilled. Frowning she shook her head. She couldn't have heard him correctly. Hope was a dragon? And what did he mean, mates? Was that like husband? Or did he mean mate, like in friend? And how could that make her a dragon?

"Ask me. I can see the questions running across your face."

"What do you mean by mates?" She groaned to herself. She should have asked about Hope. She couldn't help but hope he meant more than friends.

She'd obsessed about this man for too long as it was. So maybe he'd answer and she'd know.

"A mate is ... the other half of my soul, both human and dragon. One that makes my world complete. You are that for me." He took a deep breath. "We can change our fated mates to become dragons. Like Ari did for Hope."

"Wow." Tendrils of joy crept around her heart. Faith burrowed her head into his chest, a smile slipping over her lips. "Are you sure?"

"Yes."

"What if you're wrong?"

"I'm not."

"But what if you are?"

He snorted. "Then you won't change into a dragon."

"So, how do you do it?"

"Do what?"

She didn't believe the sudden innocence in his voice. "How would you change me into a dragon?" Faith tugged at his hair, pulling his face so he was looking at her.

"I think it would be better if I just showed you." His smile was just a bit too bright.

She glared. She would find out. Crag didn't realize quite how stubborn she could be. She snorted. He would find out.

CHAPTER TEN

Stubborn had nothing on his mate. He really didn't want to tell her. Somehow, he knew that she would not approve. It would be so much easier to show her. His nature was to act first, then apologize, if necessary.

He cringed, inwardly. It wouldn't do to show cowardice to Faith. She would hand his ass to him. She would anyway, once it was done. His smile strained his face.

Her glare cut into his soul. At least, he consoled himself, she knew that she could become a dragon. She seemed willing, eager even. Perhaps she would be fine with it.

"Well?" Demanding little thing. Her spirit larger than her tiny form.

"It involves pheromones." Maybe that would make her happy. He nuzzled her forehead, breathing in her scent. Intoxicating.

"That doesn't explain much."

Of course, she wasn't satisfied. A burst of pride spread through his body. Troublesome, but worthy. She would be a formidable dragon.

"Our pheromones mix. When they reach a combustible level, it will change you."

"And we haven't reached that yet?" Her quirking eyebrow left little doubt that she didn't believe him.

"I have to put out a special pheromone. I haven't yet because I didn't want to change you without your permission."

"Oh." Her features softened. She pulled his head down, her lips soft against his. "Thank you."

He groaned. The sweetness of her mouth aroused him more than he already was. She didn't realize that he couldn't really control his pheromones. They built up inside him with each encounter with his mate. Soon, whether or not she agreed, his mating instincts would trigger, drawing the other male dragons to join. The catalyst would indeed change her metabolism, ripping through her.

Faith needed to see her sister. Best to get that out of the way before he changed her.

Ari, Faith needs to see Hope.

Why?

She saw you steal her away. She has been hunting us since.

That's why she disappeared?

Partially.

What's that supposed to mean?

She was heading off on what she called an adventure.

Well, I think she found one!

He could hear the laughter in Ari's voice.

She certainly did. Crag couldn't help the grin that crept across his face.

We'll head your way. I'll let Hope know.

Rog, Hark, are you hunting? He really hoped they stocked plenty of meat. Faith would need it.

"So, can I show you? Will you accept me as your mate, become like me?" He cleared his throat. The thought alone of her agreeing roughened his voice. She had to say yes. He wouldn't be able to control himself much longer.

Be ready.

We are. Plenty of meat for a new dragoness. Hark answered through their link.

Crag could just envision his eyebrows wiggling suggestively. Subtle, his brothers were not.

I'll even wait my turn this time. Rog snickered.

Idiot had tried to eat before Hope was done feeding and been attacked for his trouble. Evidently it didn't bother him. Newly turned dragons could be testy when they thought their food was being denied them.

"Yes."

He pulled her deeper into his arms. He didn't bother answering his brothers back. Faith demanded his whole attention.

Faith opened her lips, letting him plunder her depths. A spark came alive in his chest. He hadn't really believed this mate talk his dam and sire spoke of. The tendrils of joy that filled his heart with Faith near to him were unexpected. Unexpected, but welcome.

A rush of wings around him heralded the arrival of his brothers. Hark and Rog, the pranksters settled down in a flurry of wind and wings.

She has a nice ass. Rog's eyebrows wagged up and down comically.

Shut your mouth. Crag looked around. *Go away. You'll know when I need you.*

No problem. Rog's not wrong. Hark grinned, changing smoothly into a man.

It's not like we haven't seen it all. Rog settled down rocking to create a little nest in the grass. Of course, he stayed dragon.

Go away. He didn't really think they would, but it was worth a shot.

Nope. You're going to need us soon enough. Rog's smirk had Crag grinding his teeth.

"What's wrong?" Faith pulled back, frowning.

"It's nothing." He tried to shoo his brothers away. *Go away! Before she sees you.*

"Obviously it's something." Faith tried turning to follow his gaze. He nuzzled her neck, trying to distract her.

Crag didn't know why his brothers aggravated him so much, but they did. He was pretty sure they did it on purpose.

But they were right. He would need them. Maybe even more than them. Usually it took a whole weyr. Hope's changing had taken all four of them. If it was just the three of them, he didn't know if it would work. If it didn't work, she might not believe she was his mate. He had to believe that it would work. That the three of them were enough.

Didn't you tell her you were changing her? Didn't she agree? Hark frowned.

Yes, but I didn't tell her how.

His brothers' eyes widened. Rog grinned, wide and toothy.

It might not even work. I don't know if we can even do it without the weyr.

We did it for Hope.

There were more of us.

Unless there were more dragons waking up. Crag found it hard to believe they were the last family left. He truly hoped not. Perhaps if this were not enough of an adventure for Faith, they could go searching to see if any other dragons survived the centuries.

He draped Faith's shirt across her body, hiding her from his brothers' view. The mating frenzy was one thing, having them stare at her naked body just because they could? Not happening.

Go away until you feel the call.

Fine. Rog flew away in a rush of wings.

Grinning, Hark changed and followed.

Small but strong arms pushed his head up. "What was that?"

His shoulders drooped. "My brothers landed. Being typical pests."

Faith giggled.

Crag looked at her in surprise. "I thought you'd be upset."

"I have brothers too." She kissed his nose. "Is that why you covered me?"

"Yes." Joy filled his heart. The change had to work. There was no doubt this small but ferocious woman was meant to be his. He settled, distributing his weight over her. "They're gone. So, where were we?"

He slid his hand down her silky abdomen, down to the heat calling him. Her soft fluff entranced him, guarding her wetness. His fingers found and lightly rubbed the bundle of nerves above her entrance. He could feel her body shake. Crag couldn't resist. He slid a finger in her heated pussy, probing the depths of her. Hot and wet, he groaned. His cock grew, hungry to seat himself home.

Faith undulated on his hand, gasping. She arched, offering her body. Crag moved, pulling off her shirt and easing her down so he could watch her expression. Adding a finger, stretching her, probing her silken depths. In response Faith tossed her head back, her body stretching in pleasure. Her nipples pebbled, a deep cherry red, begging to be suckled. Her cries speaking to his soul.

His eyes roamed, drinking in the sight before him. Just beautiful.

Hers eyes slowly opened, lazy in her passion. Her arms reaching out to drag him down.

Resisting, Crag leaned down and took a nipple in his mouth sucking hard. Sweet tasting, the nub hardened with each pull and flick of his tongue. He grasped the other between two fingers, twisting and flicking it until it stood proud, calling to him. He switched sides, wanting and aching to devour her, mark her, keep her forever.

Her moans spurring him on.

His turgid length leaping free, homed in on the slick heat between Faith's thighs. He arched, sliding in, groaning. Her body parted grudgingly, strangling him.

Faith's nails scored his back. Her heat scalding him in the best way possible.

Crag drove deeper, seating himself fully. The sound of his balls slapping against her ass with each thrust, accompanied her lusty moans. He pulled out, grunting, sliding up to rub his cock head against her clit, teasing her with short jabs.

Faith shrieked, digging her nails into his ass.

Fuck, she drove him wild. His hand slid between her thighs teasing her. Heat emanated from her, her slick petals plumb. His cocking aching to be buried in her once more. But he needed a taste. Her sweet scent making him ravenous. Her skin flushed pink with desire. He slid down, spreading her legs flat, her pink center calling to him. He dove forward, tongue spearing her. He sucked and nibbled, lapping up every drop of sweet honey. Her frantic movements drove him even deeper.

He wanted more. Calling his dragon, Crag changed his mouth, just a little. His tongue lengthened, widened, filling Faith. Her cries music to his ears. His teeth sharpened, nipping and scraping against her clit. He needed more. Her juices flowed, filling his mouth.

Her flavor enhanced to his dragon senses. He never wanted to stop.

Faith wiggled and gasped beneath him.

Crag froze.

Her hand closed over his throbbing length. Her soft, smooth fingers pulling a groan from his throat. Her slave. Hers, forever.

Abandoning her core, Crag slid up, pulling her hand away, sliding his length deep into Faith in one hard thrust. Their groans rising simultaneously. Spurred on by the noises coming from her, Crag pumped harder. His dick swelled, loving the tight, wet depths he worshiped at. Glory filled his vision. The life they could have together. The perfect fit of their bodies. Eternity together, loving and fighting and making up. All of it, the total sum of what they could be. The air permeated with the smell of sex mixed with the pine and loam from beneath them created a perfect moment in time. One he would never forget.

Faith's arms and legs wrapped around him. Crag grunted, plunging again and again into Faith. An electric spark ran the length of his spine. He would never let her go.

Faith arched, a scream breaking free, echoing around the forest. Her body seizing, trembling with the force of her release.

He was done for.

His balls drew up, his cock enlarging. Crag thrust in, his cum exploding, coating the depths of her sheath with his claim. She. *Grunt.* Was. *Grunt.* His. He stilled, breathing heavy, his cock jerking with release with each spasm of her pussy.

"You killed me." She sighed. Faith's limbs slid from him to lay practically lifeless on the ground.

He loved the soft sigh, the pure contentment in her voice.

"What a way to go." Crag sprawled across her, sated to his toes. Her chest rose and fell with each gulp of air. His head dropped, resting on the ground, his lips caressing the smooth curve of her neck. His tongue slid out, enjoying her salty taste. The shiver running up and down her body puffing up his pride.

"Off. You're too heavy." She gulped a breath, pushing feebly at his bulk.

Crag grunted and rolled, flopping onto his back. He sucked in a breath. He needed air. Beside him, Faith

113

did the same. A grin stole over his face. She was perfect. Spicy and sassy, Faith called to his dragon, setting his blood aflame. He moved his hand, seeking hers. His fingers entwined with hers. He grinned into the sky, joy stealing through his heart. She definitely belonged to him.

Laying back, staring into the sky, Crag tightened his hand. Contentment filled him when Faith squeezed back. A warm breeze stole lazily through the trees, cooling his heated flesh and drying his perspiration. Next to him, Faith shivered and curled up to his side.

She fit perfectly against him. Made just for him, thank the Fates. Her curves soft against his hardness. She nuzzled against him, burrowing into his side. His arms dragged her close, her silky soft skin entrancing him. He could lay like this forever.

The wind picked up, stirring the leaves around them. He frowned, turning his head. Amongst the trees his brothers flapped their wings, causing the breeze. The grins on their faces cried out for him to beat them. Unfortunately, he preferred to be wrapped around Faith rather than abusing his brothers.

But he wouldn't be laying there forever. Lucky for them Faith's lovely body was curled against him, hidden from their sight. He didn't feel like sharing. At some point she would become a dragon like him. That time wasn't now, not until he explained how the change would happen. It had been his intention to tell her, but he'd become distracted, overwhelmed with the scent and taste of his mate.

The wind picked up. He narrowed his eyes, starting a slight shift. He bared his teeth, threatening them. Well, as much as he could with Faith lying beside him.

Go away! His gravelly voice menacing. *Before I get up and deal with you.*

Oh, scary. Rog snickered.

Yeah. Hark nodded, his golden eyes, the eyes they all shared, gleaming. *We know you're all smoke, not fire.*

Find someone else to bother. I have a mate to woo. God give him patience. His brothers drove him to distraction. He glanced at the beauty in his arms, but not as much as she did.

CHAPTER ELEVEN

Boneless. Her limbs lay heavily against the ground. The damp earth was soft and smelled of crushed grass and moss. Mixed with the earthy aroma of the man all but surrounding her, her head swam dizzily in the intoxicating scents.

Thoughts flitted in and out of her brain, swirling in a chaotic mixture, leaving her mindless. Breathing deeply, her racing pulse settled down, one niggling thought rose above the others.

"Am I going to change now?"

The crooked grin of the man next to her, his weight cocooning her in his warmth melted her heart. She never thought her heart would be stolen. Never dreamed of dragons being part of her life. Her daydreams of adventure were much more mundane.

Her soul squealing in joy, she turned, throwing her arms around him.

"Am I?"

"No, not yet." His chest rumbled with his words, sending streaks of remembered pleasure through her.

"Soon. I want to surprise you, pleasure you beyond your imagining."

"Oh. Okay." Faith flushed. His words, the feel of his large callused hands against her back, her butt, sent heat to her core. She melted against him. Her nipples tight against his muscular chest. Nothing ever felt as good. She couldn't imagine it getting better.

"I want to go home..." Looking into his eyes as she demanded to go home, she saw a stream of emotions pass through them until they settled, looking as if frost had covered the molten gold of his eyes.

Grasping her leg, pulling it over his hip, Crag spread her for his pleasure.

"I need to..." Faith gasped feeling him impale her. She was unable to deny him anything, especially the pleasure she knew he would grant her.

His hands slid, cradling her bottom and the small of her back. Holding her against him, Crag rolled to his back. His turgid length gliding in and out of her heated passage.

He filled her. His friction calling forth more of her nectar. In and out in a dizzying pace. Her head spun.

She clenched her muscles trying to keep him in, but he slid out despite her action.

She could see a hard resolve in his eyes. She knew she should be afraid of that look but all she could think about was the rigid shaft that was making her moan and wiggle. All she cared about was the length of him spearing through her tight flesh, forging forward and back.

They rolled again, her head spinning and breath catching.

His hands grasped her buttocks and eased one finger inside her tight bottom hole. The slight burn as he breached her sent shocks of excitement zinging through her body.

Shuddering, she couldn't move. His decadent touch sending shivers up her spine. Her breasts pressed to his hard chest and her softness covered him like a blanket. Her legs spread on either side of him. She slid down, impaling herself. Now, she was filled front and back with his unrelenting heat.

Faith burned from the inside out. He owned her body and she reveled in the fact. Undulating on him, he allowed her enough room to move but not escape. Not that she wanted to. With each thrust of his penis she rubbed her clit on his abdomen, feeling it swell with each rub of his skin. Goosebumps erupted across her skin.

He snaked a hand between their bodies, fingers catching her clit and squeezing. Faith came at the sensation, coating his cock and feeling it pool at its base. Through it all he continued the unceasing rhythm inside her. She could do this forever. She panted. Forever. Her body luxuriating in her release. The sensation of his penis filling her, teasing her, winding her ever tighter, overwhelmed her.

The air surrounding them sparked, electrifying. She would never get enough. She eased on her knees, riding his cock and his finger. Harder. Being filled in both holes darkly excited her. She wanted more. She wanted it harder. Her breathing erratic. She needed more.

Looking down into Crag's golden eyes, her breath caught. His eyes were wild, his features sharp. He stared into her eyes as if he could steal her soul. She rode him, desperate for satisfaction again. His eyes widened and a feral smile crossed his face.

His hand grasped her buttocks and he smiled, teeth glinting, as he spread them wide. Faith's eyes widened as she felt something harder and wider than his finger enter her ass.

She gasped, throwing her head back. Crag's hands still spread her, holding her open for whatever invaded her. Hands grasped her breasts squeezing them almost painfully. Offering up her nipples to Crag's mouth. He opened up and latched on to her breast suckling. His tongue circling her nipple. Flicking it until it was hard as a rock.

Faith bowed her body, screaming at the pleasure streaking through her. Crag filled her pussy; another cock filled her ass. Crag's mouth suckled on her breast. A breast held up for him by another hand. Suddenly another mouth latched on to her other breast, pulling her deeply into another hot, wet mouth. A hand snaked down her belly leaving her shivering in its wake.

Circling her belly button, dipping in and out, then sliding down, making its goal obvious. It pressed her clit, forcing its way down to her hood. Rubbing a callused finger against her sensitive nerve endings, circling her tingling bit of flesh. Faith keened, her body a mass of sensation.

The slide in and out, hard and slick, of Crag in her pussy a biting pain in her ass thrilling her darker side, and her sensitive clit manipulated until she squeezed the cocks inside her. A screaming, breaking pleasure filled her. Teeth nibbled, pulling on her nipples. Fingers squeezed her clit, pinching her, making her scream again. Faith exploded, strangling the cocks that filled her. Cum burned, heated almost beyond her ability to endure, ass and pussy filled while she screamed. A dick was thrust into her open mouth. She suckled, desperate for more.

She cried out. They shifted her, ass and pussy now empty. She suckled harder, wanting more. A groan erupted from above her and the penis in her mouth throbbed. Cum poured down her throat. She sobbed desperately, while trying to swallow every bit. Withdrawn from her seeking mouth, suddenly her pussy was stuffed full. Moaning she arched to take every bit. She felt wild.

Crag slammed into her from behind. Her ass raising with each thrust. She looked up and another cock filled her mouth, muffling her moans. A head slid under her belly and the hot breath of a mouth touched her pussy even as it was being rammed. A tongue reached out and licked delicately at her clit before moving closer and suckling it. Suckling it until she screamed and squeezed the cock in her pussy. She could feel herself throb and release, desperately seeking more. More pleasure, more everything. Everything they could give her.

It wasn't enough. Her brain, her body in a frenzy, she wanted, needed more.

Faith was lifted and turned. Settled down on her back on top of a man whose dick was rising in the air between her pussy lips. Her legs thrust towards her stomach. He guided himself into her ass.

Faith moaned, the decadent slide of hard steel into her tight, silken depths driving her wild. Faith didn't care that at this point she was naked with her legs spread and her pussy wide open to anyone that came by. She could feel her clit throb, demanding attention. She grasped her legs around the knees and spread them, offering her pussy to be filled. "Please."

She undulated, breathing deeply, her ass filled, the pleasure and pain so intense her soul flew. She spread her legs and thrust her boobs in the air. She screamed, her pussy filled before the first cock finished settling into her ass. Mouth open, breathing deeply, she panted, mind in a whirl.

She opened her mouth, wanting to taste, to suck. Her silent demand was answered. A thick, fat cock rammed into her mouth choking her.

"So pretty. Her pussy so red and glistening."

"It feels so much better than it looks." The harsh breathing of the man above her, the feel of his foreign cock grinding in her pussy drove her wild.

"And her nipples, look at how hard they are, so sweet."

Lips suckled her nipples, nibbling, making her thrust, and riding the cocks filling her. She moved her arms dropping her legs to the ground as she grasped the head that was nibbling on her breasts and held it to her. Chuckles reverberated, making her nipples even harder.

"Please. Please." The words garbled, spilling from her full mouth. Faith spread her legs wider. The cock in her pussy torn away. She looked up at a growled "mine". Her pussy liquid, dripping her scent, calling to him. Hers, she wanted hers. Needed Crag with a desperation she'd never known.

Faith gasped. His mouth latched on her, sucking and filling her with his tongue, then delicately teasing her clit.

"Mine." Crag bit her clit, making her scream and jerk. Her ass squeezed. A groan came from beneath her. Crag lifted her up, the cold the breeze blowing on her hot, steaming pussy. His hands were on her hips, hard and tight. He thrust inside her. She jerked in a scream. She hadn't felt so full. He held her still, ramming into her. One hand sliding down to pluck at her clit as the mouth on her breast sucked harder and harder, her body spasming.

Filled above and below, her body nothing but a willing vessel for their pleasure. Faith screamed, a radiance so pure washing through her. Jerking rhythmically on the cocks stuffing her, she came and came, unaware they filled her with their cum. Only knowing that somehow, someway, in the blush of her satisfaction that she would never be the same.

CHAPTER TWELVE

Crag gazed at her in satisfaction. She was his now. He had no idea where the other dragon had come from. His brothers had been waiting, knowing Crag intended on mating Faith. The other dragon must have been drawn by Faith's pheromones. He rejoiced their clan wasn't the only one left.

He looked at his brothers and the other dragon.

"Hunt." He looked at Faith. "She'll be hungry." Crag looked at them.

They were looking down at Faith in satisfaction, adding another mate to the fold to build their weyr stronger and repopulate their race was no small thing.

"Now. Or do you want to face a hungry, angry dragoness?"

They changed leaping into the sky to hunt.

You do realize that we already have meat available. Hark remarked.

Let's bring it back, then I'll start a fire. Rog added.

The unknown dragon nodded, following his brothers into the sky.

Thank you.

Crag leaned over and gathered Faith into his arms. She curled into him, exhaustion in every line of her body.

"I've never felt so overwhelmed before." She snuggled further into his arms, her curves pressing softly against him.

"That was our mating ritual. When the pheromones get to a certain peak there is no turning back."

"I just know that it took four men to satisfy me. How can that be? How often is that going to happen?" Faith frowned.

"You're mine. That will never happen again. It only happens to build enough power for the change. It takes the weyr to do that." He was striding towards the river as they talked. He entered the water going deeper until just their heads were above water. "Hold on to my neck."

Faith slid her arms tighter around his neck. Squeaking a bit as his hands dropped and she floated, held in place by only her arms. His hands ran up and down her body rinsing her off.

"I'll be back in a second." Crag ducked under the water.

Faith sank down, floating in the water. Crag slid back up until her arms were once again around his neck.

"What were you doing?"

"Getting this." Crag ran his hands all over her again this time with sand to help rub her clean. "This should help get rid of the stickiness. And remove the scent of the other dragons from you."

Faith raised an arm, sniffing it. "I don't smell."

"To a human you don't. But a dragon? You do. You smell like me, but a bit like the others. I only want my scent on you." He loved the feel of her silken skin beneath his hands.

Faith shivered in his arms, his hands sliding to clean her intimately.

Taking a deep breath, he smiled in satisfaction. Only her scent and his mingled together.

"So, does this mean I'll become a dragon?"

"Yes."

"When?" Her stomach growled.

Crag laughed. "Soon. My brothers are gathering food to help finish your change."

"You said it was a mating ritual." She peeked at him from beneath her lashes. "Am I mated to all of you?"

Crag frowned. "No. You are *mine*."

Faith was silent.

Crag could practically see her thinking. He wasn't sure about what though.

Her expressions slid across her face at a rapid pace. "Good." Her smile brilliant. "That means you are mine too."

Happiness welled up in his heart. More than he ever thought possible. "Yes, it does." He could hear the sounds of wings approaching. "Let's get out of the water. My brothers are returning. I have to find out who the strange dragon is."

Wind rushed across them, warm air drying them instantly.

Faith squealed, hands ineffectively covering her breasts and groin.

"There is a dragon right there. Will he eat me?"

"I'm pretty sure he already did." Crag flashed her wicked grin. She flushed red. He laughed, her instinctive reaction to reach out and pinch him. Lucky for him it didn't hurt. He puffed up in pride. It also showed she wasn't afraid of him.

"I don't want to walk in front of him while I'm naked."

Crag sighed. "So, I see."

This human insistence on being clothed baffled him. He preferred her naked. Hope was the same way, hiding her form. Most humans he'd met in his life were concerned with whether they had clothes on. He hoped now that Faith was his mate, she wouldn't be quite so preoccupied with it.

"He's been inside of you. What difference does it make?"

Faith stamped her foot, her arms going to her hips. Her stance spoke pure belligerence. Crag's eyes widened, watching and appreciating all her luscious bits bouncing. His loins stirring again at the sight. With her arms on her hips and her legs spread, he could once again smell her hot fragrance. The slight breeze wrapping around her tightening her nipples. He licked his lips, staring at them.

"Listen to me." Faith stamped her foot again, her breasts jiggling.

Crag wasn't sure where to look. His eyes darted between her luscious mounds and her fragrant slit. He wanted his mouth on both.

"Look at me. Not at my boobs." Faith reached out and smacked him in the shoulder.

Crag looked into her face startled. He reached his hand forward, desire rising to feel her scorching flesh.

"Oh, never mind." She turned around, bare ass jiggling, and stomped toward her bag, grumbling under her breath the whole time.

Crag just stared, entranced at all her moving flesh. His hand still reaching for her dripping pussy. He walked toward her. He wanted his mate again. He would always want her. His cock strained toward her, hitting himself in the abdomen with each stride closer.

Faith passed by the dragon and smacked him in the nose as his eyes followed her. Crag laughed at the expression on his brother's face. When Hark's tongue flicked out and smacked her in the ass, Crag couldn't help but laugh at Faiths screeching.

She turned and made a rude gesture at both to of them. She grabbed her bag and rifled through it. She pulled out what looked like a dress. A lovely cream color, too impractical for roaming the forest. She tossed it on over her head, pulling it down. It floated down just passing her knees. It settled, covering her body. She adjusted something in the back. Suddenly her breasts were cupped lovingly by the material, her hard nipples obvious through the top.

Crag swallowed. The cherry of her nipples showed if he looked hard enough, and he was. She looked like an angel, a lovely naughty angel. But her temper pushed her out of that category. Crag smirked and thanked his lucky stars. She was perfect for him just as she was.

She closed her bag, looked at the two of them and snorted. Obviously still miffed at them. She headed over toward the rock near the river and sat down. She kept both of them in her sight, like she couldn't trust either of them.

Crag turned to watched Faith settle on the rock. The sun shone behind her, giving her a lovely glow. Her curves were outlined in the sun, tempting him to touch her.

She raised her legs folding them so that she settled on the rock.

Crag's nostrils flared. From this angle he could see straight up her dress to where her legs joined. The soft luscious flesh showcased by the surrounding shadows. Her lips swollen and blushed a dark pink. They were spread as if beckoning him. Her red clit barely peeking out of its hood.

Faith squirmed beneath his stare.

He stared and watched as her pussy began to glisten. Crag could smell her arousal. He walked towards her, cock straining to enter her warmth. She began backing on the rock and Crag leaped forward and caught her, trapping her in place. He grabbed her legs and spread them, pulling her forward and spearing her on his length.

They both groaned. She felt like heaven. He shifted leaning against the rock as he pushed Faith back holding her down as he rocked and in and out of her tight, wet passage. She squeezed him each time he rammed in, her flesh pulling to keep him in as he withdrew. He sped up pounding her into the rock. He shifted a hand and let his thumb flick her clit. Her abdomen tensed beneath him. Her cry rang out. Her pussy milking him.

Crag groaned and emptied himself into her.

He pulled back looking at the picture Faith made. She lay loose across the rock arms and legs splayed. Her nipples still rock hard, straining at her top. Begging for his attention. He reached up and fingered one, circling and lightly pinching it. He could see her pussy pulse each time he did it. He bent down and buried his face between her legs, nibbling on her clit as his tongue lapped at their mixed juices, his hand busy teasing her nipples. He was rewarded each time he teased her with another burst of sweetness.

Crag sat back. One hand still working her nipple, he watched her cream. Faith wiggled in front of him. He could see her buttocks tense as she lifted her cunt towards him. He took his other hand and lightly petted her lips. Tracing around and around as they plumped up for him. He teased her clit watching it swell, holding back the little hood that hid it from his sight.

He leaned forward and blew air across it and lightly licked it. Faith's hands fluttered. Then her hands went straight to his hair pressing him down into her pussy. Crag chuckled. He felt her shiver as he did so. She arched trying to ride his face. She was so honest in her passion. Crag buried his face, his tongue licking her slick walls. Flickering up to hit that spot to drive her wild.

He succeeded.

Faith keened. Holding him by his hair as she rubbed his face into her. Her pussy clenching on his tongue as it tried to milk it. Crag scraped his teeth across her clit and Faith screamed, filling his mouth with her cum. She rode his tongue until she lay back exhausted. Crag continued to lightly lick her, cleaning her up and bringing her back down to earth.

Faith was finished, exhausted. The delicate licking of his tongue only gaining a whimper from her.

Crag sat back admiring her. Flushed a deeper red and glistening from her cum and his saliva, she lay open for his viewing. He pushed up. Leaving her there for the moment. His handiwork exposed to all who cared to look.

He turned. Hark carried a couple of deer, as did the strange dragon. They were all ready to be spitted.

"I'll start the fire." Crag headed toward his brothers.

"Looks like you already did." Rog laughed looking at Faith. "And extinguished it."

Crag shook his head at his brother's juvenile humor. One day he would be the one laughing. Rog wouldn't have a clue. He couldn't wait.

Crag looked up. Faith was watching him and Hark. Unbeknownst to him, she had managed to pull her dress back into place. When she saw him looking at her, she slid off the rock and headed toward him. He held out an arm to see if she would come to him. She smiled, ducked under his arm, and snuggled into his side.

With Faith in his arms, he turned to the unknown dragon. He was large but not any larger than him and his brothers. He was also eying Faith closer than Crag liked.

"I am Crag Sarkany." He gestured to his brothers. "My brothers Hark and Rog, and you've met my mate, Faith. And you are?"

The other dragon, a pure white in color looked at him and rumbled. He changed and stepped forward, a tall and lanky man. Younger than Crag expected, but his hair was as white as his scales.

"I am Blanc Nuage."

"And where are you from? I don't recall ever seeing you around here."

"I am not from here. I, along with a few others from my weyr, are traveling." He held out his hand to shake Crag's. "I am from the Québec province in Canada. We live in the mountains just a bit north of Québec city." He eyed Crag and his brothers, looking at them curiously.

"Then I take it you're not staying. We live in the mountains not far from here."

"You are fire dragons, yes? We are ice dragons. We came down to see if this land looks like ours."

"Yes, we are." Crag grinned at him. "I've never met an ice dragon before. I've heard of them." Crag shrugged. "Just never met one before. What do you mean looks like yours?"

"Very little of the human population around us survived. At least on this continent. How far have you explored?"

Crag sighed. "Not much. But there are very few humans left, nothing like I remember from my last awakening. How much have you explored?"

"We flew to the coast closest to us and then turned west. The earth has reclaimed itself, covering the ravages of man. We saw very few humans."

"My mate's village is one of the only ones we have seen. But there are others. They've told us of others visiting them and they also mentioned a few villages that they can travel to in a few days. So, there are some left."

Blanc looked at Faith. "My brothers and I are looking for female dragons. I would like to take this one back."

Crag stood taller pulling Faith tighter into his side. He could feel his dragon bristle, ready to challenge the other.

"This one is my mate. You cannot have her. You know that. You helped perform the mating ritual." His voice was hard as he glared at the dragon. He could see his brothers shifting behind him, backing him up.

Blanc put his hands up in a placating gesture. "That is fine. I was just checking. I wasn't sure it was a mating ritual or you were just making use of this human."

Crag heard Faith gasp and she buried her head in his side.

"No, she is my mate." He frowned at Blanc. "Don't you get mating urges? All of my senses point only to one mate. Not just any woman would do. Isn't it the same for an ice dragon?"

Blanc sighed and looked down. "I don't know. When we woke up all the elders were gone. Our dam and sire, gone. No one left except for myself and the other young ones that had just awakened. I had the need to head in this direction. We all did."

"How many came with you? You said you all did, but how many is that?"

"There were five of us. Five old enough to go on the hunt. We split a while back, each of us following a different path. Mine drew me here." He looked at Faith. "I believe it drew me to her. She must be my mate, not yours."

Crag shook his head violently. "No, she is not. She is my mate. Tell me, do you still feel an urge that you can't explain?"

Blanc frowned as he thought about it. The clearing by the river was quiet as he obviously mulled over his answer. He lifted his head and looked at Crag.

"Yes. I do. Do you think that means my mate is out there?"

"Yes. That is what we were taught by our dam and sire. And for my brother Ari and myself it has turned out true. Our instincts brought us to our mates."

Crag settled back leaning against a tree. Blanc looked confused and paced back and forth in front of him.

"I don't understand. If she is your mate," Blanc gestured at Faith, "why is it you shared her with so many other dragons?"

Crag's jaw dropped open. He could see the surprise looks on his brothers' faces also.

"Don't you have anyone to teach you? How long have you all been alone? Most mates are human. You have to have found *your* true mate to be able to turn them into a dragon, and when you have found her, or him, you need the combined sexual chemistry from the weyr to change them. If you don't, they will never become dragons."

Crag could feel Faith elbow him.

"That's the part you left out." She whispered. Her glare warred with the satisfaction in her eyes.

He leaned down, kissing the tip of her nose. "Because I need you, my mate."

"When will I change?"

Crag could hear his brother's chuckle behind him. They had seen how aggravated Hope became when she was changed without notice. At least Faith knew it was coming.

"It's different for everyone. Different things set it off. Hunger is usually the main one or aggravation or even desire. Extreme emotions seemed to set up the first change." Crag shrugged. "Like I said, it's different for everyone. We have not had mates join the weyr in many years. When we were younger, we really didn't pay much attention."

"Enough. I need answers." Blanc interrupted. "Do you mean to tell me that you have to have multiple dragons to change our mates?" Crag and his brothers nodded their heads. "And it has to be your true mate?"

"Yes. If it's not your true mate, you'll not be able to reach the peak required to set off the mating ritual." Crag could feel Faith's head bounce back and forth as she took in the information. Luckily for the most part she was quiet.

"So, just taking any woman will not work."

Crag shook his head. "No, it will not. You will not be able to generate or complete the change. If you can do neither, you will die out. You can only have hatchlings with your true mate."

"Do you think he can get dressed?" Faith whispered, nodding toward Blanc. The dragons laughed. It was obvious they all heard her.

"Yes, I can." Blanc bowed to Faith. He turned and strode over to the river. Leaning over he picked up the bag similar to Crag's. He pulled out a pair of trousers, donning them.

She had been trying to keep her eyes on his face. Crag couldn't help but chuckle. Humans were so conscious about nudity. It seemed an odd quirk considering all of them had been inside her. He wasn't sure he would ever understand the human mind. Faith released a sigh once he was clothed.

"I think you should get dressed too."

Crag laughed. "Later."

He started as a pair of pants hit him in the back of the head. They dropped to the ground in a billow of dust.

Faith giggled, tugging a reluctant smile to his face.

"Fine. But that means the rest of you better get dressed, too." Crag looked over her shoulders. Hark was standing there with a grin on his face and already dressed.

"Already took care of it." Rog spitted a deer, placing it over the fire.

Blanc walked back over to the group.

"I don't understand. I was drawn here, yet I still feel an urge to move on. When I saw her, I thought she was my mate. I couldn't turn away from her. Why is that?" He stood facing Crag, his stance belligerent. "How do I know you're not lying to me?"

"That's because the mating ritual had started. If no other dragons had been around it would've just been some really hot sex. But when our pheromones mix with our fated mates, it spreads. It draws all dragons within the area to participate."

"So, any dragon in the area would've responded."

"Yes, any unmated dragon. The pheromones will not affect those that are mated." Crag grinned. "If it did the mated dragon would be in a sorry state. You never want to offend a dragoness. Her bite may not be lethal but you'd wish it were."

"So, if I had found my mate, I wouldn't have been affected?"

"No. Not if you had completed the mating ritual with her."

"This is all so confusing. None of us have learned all this. Are you sure this isn't only for fire dragons?"

"No." Crag shook his head. "It is for all dragons. Our elders are very clear on that."

"We need this knowledge. Can you help us?" Blanc put his hands out in supplication. "We have no one to teach us."

Crag sighed, debating. He couldn't just let a whole race of dragons die. There were plenty of elders in the clan that would be willing to help.

"Stay with us. We have plenty of elders that would be willing to teach you. Some might even be willing to go back with you to your clan. I just have to contact them."

"Thank you." A smile broke out on Blanc's face. "I can't thank you enough. I need to find the rest of my group. Would you be willing to stay here so I can gather them?"

"Yes." Crag nodded. "That would not be a problem. We can stay here day or two waiting."

"I will try to contact them first. If not, I will have to go to them." Blanc turned away his body more relaxed than Crag had seen it. He realized that getting answers was more important to Blanc than he had realized. Perhaps he didn't want to tell them how bad their situation really was.

Crag watched Blanc walk away and cock his head. It was obvious from his posture that he was trying to communicate with the other dragons. He could catch none of it. Not surprising since they had no blood bond. He turned and pulled Faith against him. Blanc wasn't his first concern.

"Hark, Rog, can you stay? I don't know exactly what's going on with Blanc and his dragons, but I don't want to be left alone with Faith. She's too vulnerable at the moment."

"Give it a day or so, she won't be." Rog grumbled under his breath.

Hark snorted, adding to Crag's amusement.

"Sure. You know that's no problem. Did you want to see if Ari wanted to come? God knows Hope likes causing trouble. She'd be sure to join in if there was a fight." Hark laughed.

They all flashed quick grins. Hope had proved she was a hothead. It went right along with the copper streaks in her hair.

"I had already asked him to come. So that Faith can see Hope is okay, and I wasn't lying to her." He leaned over and kissed the top of her head.

"Thank you." She embraced his waist, resting her head against his heart.

"Hark, can you reach anyone at home from this distance?" He tightened his arms around her. He never wanted to let her go.

For all their mind speak capabilities, distance could be an issue. Crag wasn't sure exactly how far they were from home and if they would still be able to reach their sire. Ari wasn't too far but Hope still hadn't gotten the hang of mind speak. Crag wasn't sure if she knew she what it was. Hark seem to have the best capability of distance. The location of Crag and Ari's new weyr was because it was within distance of the clan using mind speak. But far enough away from their sire's territory to give them independence.

Faith was quiet. It made him wonder if she was just tired or if she was thinking. Crag much preferred to think that she was tired. He already learned a thinking Faith was trouble.

CHAPTER THIRTEEN

Faith smoothed her cheek against Crag's chest. The sound of his steady heartbeat was soothing. Cradled in Crag's arms, his warm strength surrounded her gave her a sense of protection. His skin soft to her touch yet with an underlying hardness like rock.

Her breath caught in her throat when the new dragon stated he wanted to take her with him. Fear streaked along her nerves, when she thought that Crag would say yes.

Instead he had pulled her tight and flatly refused the other man. She wanted to melt into his body. Crag made her feel loved and wanted. She was not interchangeable. He cherished her. It showed in his every touch. Could she still leave? Wasn't he offering her the adventure of a lifetime?

Crag ran his hand up and down her back, carrying on a conversation with his brothers. He didn't even seem aware he was doing it, an unconscious, affectionate gesture.

Faith burrowed into him, letting the conversation flow on around her. She didn't need to worry. His warmth blanketed her.

It wasn't the spark that seemed to flare every time they even looked at each other that made her waver on the decision to leave him. It was moments like these, when he reacted without even thinking about it, which made the thought of no longer being by his side impossible to even think of.

Faith sighed, contentment leaching into her bones. This man, this dragon, was the adventure of a lifetime.

The smell of roasting meat had her lifting her head. Sniffing, her stomach growled. Saliva pooled in her mouth. "I'm hungry."

The men turned and looked at her. She knew her tone of voice hadn't been the nicest but she couldn't seem to help herself. Her stomach felt like it was eating itself from the inside out. She needed food and she needed it now. "Now." She turned to look at the deer and back at them. "And don't ruin the hides I want them."

The one on the spit was done for, but she could make them save the rest.

They all had big grins on their faces. All four men, Blanc included, responded to her demand. She had never had anyone listen to her like that before. Faith smirked. She could get used to it.

Faith had never felt so hungry. The gurgling in her gut tearing her to pieces. She'd bite the raw venison soon if it didn't cook. She watched in approval as Crag sliced a thick steak from the deer in front of him. He placed it in the fire to sear it. His brother continued to rotate the deer on the spit. Crag was slicing more of the deer into steaks and setting them in the fire. The smell of roasting venison drifted to her nostrils.

Faith's eyes blurred and when she opened them, her world appeared to have shifted.

"Open up, Faith." She looked at Crag, then opening her mouth when the scent of the steak reached her nostrils. Her stomach rumbled again. She had never been so hungry.

Crag tossed a steak into her mouth.

Faith quickly chewed it and opened her mouth for another. They seemed smaller than expected. She looked at the spit. Hark was slicing the deer into steaks and handing them to Crag to place in the fire. They barely seared before she demanded more.

Her middle lay hollow, growling despite each bite. The deer really didn't look that big anymore. She wondered if the fire was shrinking it. No way could that little hunk of meat fill her up. She shook her head. No, those were really big deer, she'd seen the dragons drop them. They seemed tiny now. The ache in her middle demanded more. She reached out and grabbed the deer on the spit, munching the semi-cooked meat, the flavor melting on her tongue.

She heard the men laugh. She. Did. Not. Care. No matter how appalling her behavior was, if she really thought about it. The growling of her belly superseded any worry about manners. The taste of the venison sliding down her throat made her tummy rumble in contentment. The coppery taste of blood in her mouth against the tough flesh of the deer was a contrast in flavors and textures that exploded in her mouth. Venison never tasted so good. Savoring it, Faith snapped her eyes open when it was gone. She wanted more.

Crag must have read her mind. He tossed her more steak. She quickly gobbled them down. One brother finished stripping the hide off the deer tossing it to Crag who put it over the fire. Faith waited impatiently. The smell of the blood and the raw flesh was appetizing in an icky kind of way, if she thought about it. When the carcass was brown from the flame, Faith snatched it out of the fire with her jaws. She contentedly munched while eyeing up another.

"Hark go hunting." Crag said. He turned to Blanc. "Will you help him? I don't think we have enough." Blanc nodded and strode away stripping his pants off, leaping into the sky, changing into a pure white dragon. Rising higher, she noticed his belly was a sky blue. If she hadn't watched him, he would have disappeared, blending into the sky. She sniffed, turning her head back towards Crag and the overpowering smell of meat.

He was the one that smelled so good to her. *Mine. Mate. Hungry.* Her thoughts were primitive. Faith frowned. A bit primitive even for her. Her hunger overrode all thought processes though. She needed more food. Crag finished stripping the skin off the final deer.

She sniffed around the fire and found a few steaks that hadn't been given to her. She quickly snapped them up, chewing contentedly while she eyed the final deer. She watched each move Crag made. Not willing to share her food. At all. The men would find that out quickly if they tried to take it.

Crag looked at her and the deer that she was eyeing. He smiled and tossed it to her. Faith snatched it out of the air as he tossed it toward her. She crunched and felt the gratifying destruction of bone and the warm spurt of blood down her throat. The stringy flesh gave her a sense of satisfaction as she chewed. She sighed, enjoying the sensation.

She looked around at her final mouthful. Her stomach was still growling in hunger. She eyed the men. They were supposed to provide for her. Her mate stood in front of her empty-handed. Faith rumbled in dissatisfaction. Her emotions swirled. Why were they not feeding her?

A deer landed in front of her face from above. She jumped back, startled.

Crag laughed.

Faith glared, too hungry to snap at him. She snatched the deer, filling her mouth. She chewed and chewed. The crush of bone and taste of blood soothing her. Another fell and another, landing within easy distance. She preened. That was better. They should be taking care of her needs. One of men made as if to grab one and she snarled, pulling the carcass closer to her. Hers, the meat was hers.

Crag snickered and the other stepped back, laughing. He turned and spoke. Faith didn't hear it over the crunching in her mouth. She liked the sound of the snap of bones in her ears. She knew something wasn't normal. She didn't feel like herself, yet she felt more alive than she ever had before.

She guessed the mating ritual succeeded. That didn't mean she would focus on what she looked like now. Focusing on filling her empty belly became her priority. Her emotions swung wildly. What would she look like? Would she still be herself? Would the emotions coursing through her veins change her into a creature that only reacted, that didn't think? She cringed at the possible answer.

The grass beneath her was soft. She could smell the scent of the leaves and that peculiar smell that wet stones have. The dirt had a flavor and feel all its own. It felt cool beneath her feet, coating her toes as she dug them in. She tasted dirt on the flesh of the animals she devoured.

She could tell where each person was. Their individual scents giving away their positions. She purred, inching closer to her mate. Crag smelled like hers. Faith nosed the carcass in front of her. She daintily took it between her teeth tearing the flesh from the bones. She chewed contentedly, eating until her stomach filled. Regretfully eyeing the deer still laying there. There. Was. No. More. Room. She burped daintily and settled down, relaxing.

Now, she needed to see. Stretching out an arm, her eyes widened in surprise. Iridescent scales covered a limb. Not really an arm anymore. A muscled limb, topped off by a claw with deadly looking, she peered closer, blue talons. Not any blue, but turquoise. Shifting her limb, okay, leg, it gleamed. White, but not. Flashes of turquoise, green and a flash of fire, orange sparkled from it.

Turning her head, looking over her huge body, turning her head this way and that, Faith couldn't help grinning. She was beautiful! She gleamed. Each movement flashing hidden colors. She stilled, her head watching her body. A shimmery white settled, her scales camouflaging the colors. Twitching her back, raising her wings, the movement brought out all colors of the rainbow.

She grinned. Being a dragon was awesome!

CHAPTER FOURTEEN

Crag laughed. He leaned over and kissed Faith between her nostrils. He took the deer and quickly put it on the spit. Faith was preening over her new form and she either didn't care or didn't notice.

Crag looked at Faith. A miniature dragon, a gorgeous beauty, all his. A pocket dragon, he'd named her sister. Faith changed into a similar size. Her scales were beautiful. A deep coppery color near their root changed to an iridescent white gleaming with all colors of the rainbow when she moved. His heart beat erratically, gazing at her. She was all his.

Hark and Blanc landed, tearing his attention their way.

They brought a couple more deer each, enough to satisfy everyone's hunger. He knew they had eaten on the hunt. That's normally the way they did it. There was no use going hungry if you didn't have to. However, they made sure that they always provided for those that remained behind to guard something precious. A new dragon, a new mate, was more precious than anything in the world.

Crag didn't like the way that Blanc was eyeing Faith. He appeared too interested in her. Blanc turned towards him.

"She could be an Ice Dragon. Look at the white of her scales. She doesn't look like any fire dragon I've ever heard of."

"She is mine. Look at her base. She is copper, pure fire under all those white scales. Don't even think she's not full of fire. It wouldn't matter what she was. She is mine."

"I'm just saying, she looks like an ice dragon."

Crag eyed Blanc. He didn't say anything, just stared until Blanc backed down. No one questioned what was his. Especially not some dragon that knew nothing about his own species. Or so he said. Crag wondered how ignorant the rest of the group was. Or was it an act? He just couldn't trust him.

"Did you reach the rest of your clan? Are they coming?"

"Yes, they are. They should be here tomorrow. Will we wait for them to arrive?"

"Yes. We will wait. You all need education on our species. I don't understand what happened to your elders, but my clan will help."

"Thank you. We appreciate it." The humility Blanc showed seemed fake. Crag bristled, his tone belying his words. It might be nothing more than Blanc grudgingly showing gratitude, but better safe than sorry.

"How many of your clan is coming? You said there were five or six of you searching."

"I only reached one, he contacted the others. They will be here."

Crag contemplated his words and body language. He did not trust Blanc any more than Blanc trusted him, his distrust shining from his expression. Perhaps they thought they were the only dragons left and Crag and his brothers were a rude surprise. Or it could be something more nefarious. Only time would tell.

Looking at the evidence of the youth in Blanc's eyes, he shrugged. Young pride, perhaps. Blanc looked like a fully grown human, but his dragon showed the fact he was indeed a youth. If he aged in at a hundred,

Crag would be surprised. Young dragons could be very stupid.

Point in case, they were hunting women. Whether their deeds showed a lack of knowledge or indeed nefarious purposes, his clan would put a stop to it. It was actions like those that caused the humans to hunt them down in centuries past. The decimation of the human race was a new opportunity to begin again without worries. Stealing women would once again bring down the human's wrath on dragons. No matter how few of them were around.

"You can't steal women. You can take your mates, but that will just get you a pissed off dragoness. Try not to do that if you have a choice. Too many times in the past, humans gathered together to wipe clans out. The only ones we take are our mates, and we make sure the families are okay with it." He snickered. "Usually we convince the women and their families reluctantly agree."

Blanc looked at him shaking his head. "You tell the humans you are dragons?"

"No. Only under extreme circumstances." He turned at the sound of Rog's laughter. "Why are you

159

laughing?" He felt a sinking suspicion in his gut. "What did Hope do? Or should I ask what did you goad Hope to do?"

"Not me!" He turned to Hark. "Tell him. I had nothing to do with it." Rog turned to Crag. "I wasn't even around. It was all Hope's doing." He was grinning from ear to ear.

Hark tried to stifle his laughter but not successfully.

"You might as well tell me." Crag could feel his jaw clench as he shook his head in disgust. He just knew he wasn't going to like what he heard.

"We already told you Hope's family knows. We just didn't tell you how."

"You said the whole family came running. Exactly what did she do?"

"Hope decided that her grandmother needed to know. She took her out to the barn and changed in front of her. It set her grandmother screaming and beating her with the broom. Everyone came running to see what was going on." Rog shook in laughter. "It was the funniest thing I've ever seen. If anyone deserves to have their ass beat by a broom, it's Hope."

Crag shook his head. He witnessed Rog and Hope's behavior. Two little kids in a playground goading each other into misbehaving. Of course, he would find it funny.

Crag took a deep breath, trying to stop his growl. Fury thrummed in his veins. Breathing deeply, he tried calming down. Heat streamed up his neck, turning it red. His muscles trembled in anger. He took another deep breath.

That grandmother was not safe. She knew before Hope told her. She hated them. Crag bristled, remembering the depth of her hatred. It flowed from her every pore. Maybe Hope could change that. If not, Crag would have to eliminate her for his family's protection.

He felt the touch of Faith's snout against him. She rubbed his chest, trying to sooth him, her tongue sneaking out to flick his cheek. His anger dissipated at her touch. His lips twitched. Her scales were soft and pliable, but her tongue wet. He glanced at the amusement in her eyes. And deliberately slobbery. Her snicker confirmed it. He gently shoved her face away, focusing on Hark's words.

"Crag, it's okay. Ari and Henry were discussing moving the family out to your land. Henry agreed to come check it out. See if it was suitable for the family, when Hope pulled that stunt." Hark shook his head. "It was funny as hell. She stood there, wailing. She changed and realized she ruined her dress. I think she cried harder about the dress than the beating her grandmother gave her."

"Yep. There's definitely something wrong with that woman. I think Ari should beat her every day." Rog had a huge grin on his face. Crag knew he and Hope had bonded in an odd kind of friendship. Partners in mischief. He protected her when Ari wasn't available. It would be interesting to see the mate that fate had in store for him.

"What is he talking about? What's the matter with Hope? Why was grandmother beating her? Hope is her favorite. And how do I change back? I don't even know how I shifted into a dragon in the first place." She looked beseechingly at Crag. "I did become a dragon, didn't I? Oh God, how can I change back?" Her expression became frantic.

"You were hungry. There is nothing wrong with your sister. Now that your hunger is satisfied, think about being human again. You'll change back."

"Will that always happen when I'm hungry?" Faith looked appalled. "That would not be good." Crag couldn't help but laugh, despite the news about the grandmother.

"No. For the most part you should be able to control your change. The first one is usually set off by hunger or another strong emotion. After that it's up to you." He grinned anticipating how the next sentence would set her off. "Except for one instance. Your mate can force a change on you. Which means I can make you change. Usually for your own good or your safety." He grinned. "Sometimes a dragoness has more fierceness than common sense."

Faith's eyes narrowed and her lip pulled back in a snarl. "Don't you ever dare to force a change on me!"

He laughed at her reaction. Crag wasn't wrong in his guess, her temper lit up at the information. Grinning he placed a noisy kiss on her snout. "I won't if you behave." He jumped back, avoiding her teeth when she snapped at him. He chuckled.

"Now, now, it's that type of behavior that will get you changed."

He probably shouldn't have said that. Faith instinctively knew how to use her tail as a weapon, swiping at him before he knew it. His legs flew out from beneath him and he landed on his back on the hard ground. His breath exploding from his chest. Sucking air back into his lungs he started choking on the dirt in the air. He couldn't stop laughing between his coughs. If it had been dirt instead of grass, he believed there would've been a bigger poof of dust as he landed. As it was, a small dust cloud billowed from beneath him.

He knew she wouldn't like his remark, but he couldn't resist. He definitely liked tweaking her tail. Crag struggled to his feet, wheezing with amusement, while avoiding Faith's tail, still twitching with her ire.

Glaring at him, Faith snorted and stomped over to the water. Tail wagging in a snit behind her. Crag didn't mind. He turned his head to watch her go. Dragon or human, he liked to watch her wag her back end. She looked at the river, glanced back at him and jumped in. Crag didn't worry too much, dragons were very good swimmers. She splashed around coming out with her scales sparkling and teeth gleaming with her smile. At least her temper sparked fast and short.

Hark and Rog were still laughing, whether over Hope's or Faith's antics he didn't know. They were cleaning and roasting the rest of the deer so were not causing mischief so Crag didn't have to worry about them.

Faith splashed out of the water and shook. She changed there on the riverbank with the sun shining down on her milky white body. She realized what she had done and squealed, diving behind a rock and grabbing her bag.

Crag enjoyed the view but realized that, unfortunately, so had all the other dragons with him. He snarled at them, warning them off. His brothers laughed but Blanc just raised an eyebrow.

Faith came out from behind the rock wearing another dress. This one floated loosely around her body, accentuating each curve it came into contact with as she walked. Crag swallowed. He could feel his pants, once again, get tight. The snickers from his brothers let him know his problem obviously showed. He ground his teeth. He wished he was the only hatchling his parents had.

He strode toward Faith, grabbing her hands and pulling her into his arms. "You are beautiful, your dragon and your woman. I'm glad you are mine." He kissed her.

Faith's warm, sensuous curves molded to his frame. His pulse picked up, her heat exciting him. Her human form seduced him, pulling emotions out he would prefer to ignore. He couldn't though. He couldn't ignore his mate.

She became the center of his world. Her dragon, sparkling and iridescent, held sexy under tones of a rich fire orange. Fire calling to him, licking through his veins, burning up his soul. He would protect his mate with every breath in his body.

He tightened his arms around her, eyeing up the unknown dragon. His brothers might tease him, but they were safe. Blanc on the other hand, bothered him.

Blanc's interest in Faith set his scales on edge. Trust didn't come easy, and the other dragon kept his nerves on edge.

Blanc kept looking at Faith from the corner of his eyes. His interest in her, despite his protests to the contrary, meant he needed to be watched. Luckily both Hark and Rog would be able to keep an eye on him. Even now they conversed with him, dragging his attention back toward them.

Crag's chest vibrated with the need to keep his growl inside. He glanced down. Faith yawned and snuggled against him. A bubble of happiness lit within his chest, bringing a smile to his face.

She was all his.

CHAPTER FIFTEEN

Faith yawned. Tired to her toes, today felt like it would never end. Closing her eyes, she sank into Crag's arms.

He ran a hand slowly through her hair. His caress turning her near boneless.

Moaning, she relaxed further. She could have sworn he growled, but she didn't see any threat.

Just the other dragons. Her face burned, embarrassed to her toes. All well-built men, and each of them handsome in their own way. She refused to think about how she was changed. It just better not ever happen again. From Crag's possessiveness she doubted it would.

She peeked up at Crag's strong jaw. They were not nearly as handsome as him, though. Her eyelids drooped. It didn't matter what time it was, sleep crept over her, dousing her concern. Crag would protect her.

"Tired?" His soft whisper in her ear brought a smile to her mouth.

"Yes." She yawned, glancing at him, realizing she opened her eyes to reply. "Yes. Very." Laughing, she continued. "More than I can believe."

Crag swept her into his arms. "Then it's time for bed."

Faith screeched, clamping her arms around his neck.

"Give a girl a warning next time." Having no energy to protest, her eyes drooping, and her belly full, Faith snuggled into his neck.

Warm and safe, his chuckle followed her into sleep.

Faith woke hours later. At least, it seemed hours later. The fire died down, only the glowing embers lit. Lumps on the ground showed the other dragons nearby. Crag snuggled up behind her, arms protectively surrounding her. Her face burned, she could feel skin against skin. Wiggling, she realized at least they were under a blanket of sorts.

The sky, a weird color, belonged between midnight and dawn. That time of day between deep slumber and early morning chores.

Her bladder pressed insistently, leaving Faith in no doubt of why she awoke. Wiggling, she eased out from beneath Crag. The tree line beckoning her urgent need. Crawling out from his welcoming arms, she stood. Looking around she spied her dress. Stretching, she hurriedly slid it over her head, hoping no one else woke. Her need urgent, Faith ran awkwardly toward the shelter of the trees.

Away from the men, hiding to take care of business, she sighed in relief. Standing up, stepping away, her dress settled back down as it swirled around her legs. The caress sending echoes of Crag's touch to her core. Her nostrils flared at the ache. A shiver shimmied up her spine.

Her stomach rumbled, reminding her of the banked fire. Breakfast, mmm. The thought of roasted meat making her drool, but the fire required a bit of flame. Looking around, gathering fallen branches on her return path, Faith headed back to the man who occupied her thoughts.

Arms full, she dropped the load she'd accumulated next to the fire. Three bodies jumped at the noise. One chuckled. Crag. Smirking his way, Faith guessed he woke when she slipped out of his arms.

"I'm hungry."

Crag's brothers glanced at each other, yawning and shaking their heads.

"So that means we need to hunt?" Rog's sarcastic words interrupted by another yawn. "No please?"

"I could do with some food myself. We might as well feed the newbie dragon." Hark flashed her a grin, changed and leapt into the sky.

Rog, yawning, followed him.

Faith piled logs over the dying embers, blowing to raise the flames, hoping to catch the new wood on fire.

Crag pulled Faith back into his arms, kissing her neck.

She shivered at the tingle racing down her spine.

"You're a fire dragon. Just light the fire." Crag stepped back and to her side. "Move aside and watch me."

He took a deep breath and leaning toward the fire, blew. His features shifted, changing, scales covering his face and sudden snout. Fire streamed out, setting the logs crackling.

"Wow. That's handy. But I don't know how to do that." Something inside her thrilled to the handsome dragonny man. The sight of scales twisting her nipples tight.

"Concentrate on changing just the path of your fire." Crag once again looked like the hot man she'd come to crave.

Not that the dragon wasn't attractive. At least to her dragon. She was screwed. A crook of his fingers was all he needed to make her beg in either form.

"Uh, newbie here. I don't have a path of fire." Faith rolled her eyes. Duh, she had no clue. So far, she'd become a dragon and turned back to human.

"Fine, let's start with your dragon. Concentrate, picture your dragon and change."

Faith closed her eyes, thinking of the pretty scales covering her arms. How they would gleam in the sun. Subtly, her world shifted.

"Did I do it? I think I did. Did I?" She didn't want to open her eyes to find she'd failed. She had to do this.

"Open your eyes and see." Crag's voice had deepened.

She figured he was a dragon now. Peeking, his scales gleamed in the light. His dragon smiled, teeth flashing. Instead of fear, arousal filled her. Stupid dragon. Glancing down, her pearlescent scales gleamed. Yep. Dragon. She sat up straighter.

"I did it!" Faith shimmied, grinning. She succeeded. She was going to be an awesome dragon. Her tail wagged. Oh jeez, just like a dog. Pushing that thought away, excitement filled her. She couldn't imagine a better adventure. "Show me how to make fire."

Crag ran his snout along hers, nuzzling her face and neck.

"Such a smart beauty." He stepped back. "Now, take a deep breath and…"

"Wait! Do I have to eat something special?"

"What? What do you mean?"

"To make fire. Do I have to eat charcoal? Yuck! That would be gross."

"No." Crag shook his head. "You're a fire dragon. It comes naturally."

"Are you sure?" Faith peered up at him. He stood monumentally taller than her. "Hey, how come you're so big?"

"Of course, I'm sure." He snorted at her. "Maybe because you're young. Or it could just be you're a female. Hope is tiny, too." His shrug struck her funny.

Faith laughed, or at least tried to. It came out more as a snort. She snorted some more, the crazy sounds tickling her funny bone. She took a deep breath, trying to calm down. This time her snort shot out flame instead.

"I did it!"

Crag grinned, shaking his head. "Try it again. I don't think you meant to."

The laughter in his voice aggravated her. Just a bit. She sniffed, not sure whether to be offended or prance around in excitement. Turning to the fire, Faith took a deep breath and aimed. Letting it go, she squeaked when flames came out. On command. Totally awesome.

"See, I did it! It wasn't an accident." Looking into his eyes, her belly twisted with desire. His eyes, his smile, all of him subtlety showed his pride in her. Heat behind the pride called to the lust in her.

"I knew you could." His deep voice wove deep into her psyche.

This man, this dragon changed something inside of her, called to her. She would never be the same. She was his and she knew, deep down in her bones, in the depths of her soul, that he was hers.

Thuds, something heavy hitting the ground behind her, spun her around.

Grinning, Crag's brothers landed, their prey littering the ground.

"Get to cooking, woman." Hark, she thought, spoke.

Her hackles rose. She wasn't some damn maid to wait on them. Behind her, Crag chuckled. She'd deal with him later.

"I think you need to watch yourself, brother." Maybe he wasn't laughing at her. Not if he was warning his brother.

"I'm not your maid." Flames accompanied her words.

"Cool. You've figured out your fire." Rog interjected. "Hark just meant that we share chores. If we hunt, you cook. Or we could eat it raw, either way works for us. You'll see your dragon prefers it that way."

Faith rolled her eyes. From Hark's smirk, she knew he hadn't meant it that way. Rog was right, however. The scent of the prey laying on the ground enticed her. Glancing at it, her stomach ached. A rumble had her side stepping the pair of dragons she didn't really know, inching closer to the carcasses on the ground.

They watched her, amusement gleaming from their eyes.

"We've eaten. Just grab it." Hark's teeth flashed, laughter evident in his voice.

Sniffing at him, she turned away, flouncing off toward breakfast. Faith ignored the chuckles behind her. Her stomach demanded to be fed.

CHAPTER SIXTEEN

Crag chuckled, watching Faith stick her nose in the air at his brothers' teasing. She could be a prickly little thing. The rumble in her belly attested to her hunger. Maybe it was just her appetite making her testy.

He supposed he'd see. He was well on his way to being wound around her dainty little talons. She gingerly approached the meat on the ground, cautiously glancing between his brothers and him. Hovering over one pile, she peeked back, finally settling down to nibble.

"Thank you." Ignoring the rumble in his own belly, he watched his mate, making sure she ate.

"No problem. One day you'll be hunting for us." Rog grinned.

Hark nodded along with him.

Normally Rog played the joker, but with Faith it appeared Hark took over the role of jester. It made sense for him to bond with Faith when Rog had already bonded with Hope. The bond allowed Crag an extra peace of mind.

Hark would be available to protect Faith whenever needed. Just as Rog would protect Hope if Ari wasn't around. Until Rog and Hark mated, of course. Then their attention would be all for their own mate.

Crag frowned, thinking. If Ari and he bonded with sisters, he wondered… "Do Faith and Hope have any sisters?"

"No. Thank goodness." Hark shivered.

"Don't wish any more of those females on us." Rog snarled at him. "Stubborn is not what I want in a mate."

Crag smirked. "Like you'll have a choice. Fate is probably laughing and listening, waiting just to surprise you."

His brothers growled at him, saying not a word. Probably praying to whatever gods there were to give them the type of mates they wanted.

Chuckling, Crag strutted toward the food dropped by his brothers. He loved getting the last word in. This argument went to him.

Grabbing a mouthful, he happily chomped away. Enjoying the crunch of bones, the warm meat and juices with each bite, Crag practically purred with contentment.

Next to him Faith delicately devoured her meal. She stayed in her dragon form longer than he expected. Once she finished eating, he and his brothers would show her how to fly.

A light burp, a bit of flame and a squeak from Faith pulled a chuckle from him. Glancing over, he couldn't help laughing.

Faith looked surprised and a bit embarrassed. Now that she'd discovered how to flame, it would sneak out if she wasn't careful, especially if she let it build up.

"You have to let it out periodically. If not, you stand the chance of flames erupting by accident." His grin spread over his face. Luckily, his sharp teeth didn't appear to faze Faith.

"It wasn't the fire that bothered me." She sniffed and nibbled on the charred meat in front of her.

"Okay." Well, that was clear as mud. Peeking at her from the corner of his eye, Crag shook his head. Females could be baffling.

"Why are you staring at me?" Faith glared at him from the corner of her eyes.

"You're a beautiful dragon. And you're mine." He beamed at her. She belonged to him. With him. She was his as much as he was hers.

Faith sniffed. She seemed in a bit of a mood, not that it bothered him. Now that Faith had shifted, so much more of the world opened up for them. He could take her around the world. Satisfy her desire for adventure. If becoming a dragon wasn't enough.

"When we finish, I can teach you to fly."

Faith whipped toward him, eyes wide, and a smile blooming on her snout. "Truly? That would be wonderful." She crunched, quickly devouring the animal she'd leisurely been gnawing on. "I'm done."

Crag laughed. "I'm not. Give me a minute." He quickly dispatched his meal, enchanted by her enthusiasm. "Follow me."

Faith quickly followed Crag to the river and washed, splashing water on herself, cleaning away any remnants of her meal.

Crag could hear the rumbles of his brothers. Who knows what they were going on about? The two always managed to find trouble.

He frowned, glancing around the clearing. He did not see Blanc. Something about him bothered Crag. With Blanc missing, he should be happy. But no, Blanc was the only troublesome spot in what was shaping up to be an otherwise beautiful day. Crag hadn't even heard him get up, but dragons were stealthy. He shouldn't be surprised.

"I'll be right back." He winked at Faith. "My turn to drain the snake." He chuckled when she ducked her head. Luckily a dragon couldn't blush. He'd bet anything that she'd be pink in her human form.

"Jerk."

His brothers laughed. Crag growled at them halfheartedly. Rubbing his muzzle along her shoulder, he headed into the woods. He returned shortly, drawn immediately to Faith's side. She snuggled against him. He noticed his brothers making short work of what was left of breakfast.

"I want to teach Faith how to fly when you're done."

Hark and Rog nodded, chomping happily, if a bit messily, as they ate. They looked around the clearing. Hark frowned, glancing at him.

When did Blanc leave? Hark must not have wanted to voice his concern in front of Faith. Making a big deal out of the fact that Blanc was gone would do that.

I don't know. I never heard him get up. Rog chimed in.

I don't like this. He was supposedly waiting for his dragons to come to us. Crag knew he probably shouldn't be this concerned. The situation bothered him from the beginning. Something in Blanc's story didn't ring true.

I don't either. I think we need to leave. Rog wasn't often serious, but Crag could hear in his voice that he meant it.

I agree.

What are you going to tell Faith? Hark glanced at her.

That we don't know where he went and since he left we have no reason to wait.

They nodded in agreement. Crag sucked in his gut, hoping it didn't drag on the ground and headed back to Faith. Crag nuzzled Faith, enjoying the smoothness of her scales. "Time to learn to fly. Then we'll head out."

She frowned looking around. "Aren't we waiting for Blanc? Where did he go?"

"I don't know. He left in the middle of the night without saying anything. He hasn't come back so he must have left."

"What if he's hurt?"

"It's not easy to injure a dragon. Not to mention his clan was close enough for him to talk to earlier so they would be close enough to help him if he was hurt."

Faith thought about it for a bit and nodded in agreement. "Okay. I'm ready." She shifted into her human skin, squeaking as the shift happened. She jumped behind him, hiding from his brothers. "I didn't mean to do that!"

"What were you thinking about?"

"That I needed to pack."

"What did you need to pack?"

"Just a couple of things. If I'm flying, I don't want to forget my clothes."

"Go pack up then." Crag licked her face eliciting a squeal.

"I'm naked."

He grinned. "I noticed."

Faith shoved him.

Crag wondered if she thought she could move him. "What was that for?"

"I don't want your brothers to see me."

Crag rolled his eyes. *Can you two turn around? Faith doesn't want you to see her naked.*

They didn't answer, but they turned away, their snickers drifting to him.

Assholes.

You have to admit, it is a bit ridiculous. Hark snorted.

We have already seen her naked. Rog's snicker irritated him. He was an idiot.

Just wait until you two find your mates. You'll sing a different tune.

Yeah, yeah. Now both the idiots were laughing.

His brothers were assholes. Their eggs must have been tainted. He'll have to mention it to his sire. Even his dam would have to agree.

Faith headed over to the rock her bag sat on. Pulling out a dress she dropped it over her head, concealing her form. She picked up a couple of items stuffing them in her bag. Crag saw her pull out a pouch and head to the river. She quickly filled it with water and sealed it back up. He smiled. His mate thought ahead. As a Dragon he would quickly fly to the nearest water source. She wasn't able to do that yet. She probably hadn't even thought about flying.

Shifting, Crag picked up his knapsack and slung it on.

Can we turn around now?

He glanced up. Both of the village idiots were grinning at him from over their shoulders. Maybe they'd damaged their heads opening their shells. It was the most likely explanation.

Idiots. Yes, as you can clearly see.

His brothers shifted, grabbing their bags. Faith put her bag on crosswise across her body and quickly caught him, putting her hand in his. He smiled down at her. The warmth of her hand sent contentment through his body.

Are we walking? Rog frowned.

Why can't we fly? You could always carry her you know. Hark smirked. *I'm sure she'd enjoy that.*

185

We should teach her to fly. I did teach her sister.

You dropped her sister. Crag shook his head. Rog and Hope were a dangerous combination. Two pranksters.

But she learned. Rog grinned.

Crag looked over at Faith. "Do you want to learn to fly?"

"I think I've had enough changes. Can we just walk for a bit?"

Hark heaved a big sigh.

Faith glared at him.

Rog, of course, laughed.

"Yes. It will be slower, but I'm in no hurry." Crag lifted his eyebrows, daring his brothers to say anything.

His brothers groaned, but followed along.

Hark and Rog took up the rear.

They stepped forward and were swallowed by the darkness of the woods. The bright blue sky above was dim beneath the leaves. Scattered shards lighting the way as best they could.

"We're heading toward Hope, right?"

The occasional beam of light across her face highlighted her loveliness. She shown even in the dimness of the trees.

"Yes. I understand you need to know she is okay." Crag understood she needed to see to believe. He ignored the sting from her lack of trust. It was enough that she walked hand in hand with him. Once she saw Hope, he knew that would fall away.

Ari? We're on our way. We met another dragon that left in the middle of the night. How far are you, as the dragon flies?

He hoped Ari heard him. He would know momentarily if he answered.

Maybe a half a day's flight. Why, do you expect trouble?

Maybe. Or I just might be paranoid. Only time will tell.

Just call if you have a problem. You know we'll be there if you need us.

I will. See you later today.

Crag glanced around. He didn't like the fact that Blanc left without telling anyone. He'd been suspicious of his story. Crag supposed it could happen but it stank all the way around. He hoped he was wrong. If he was, his clan would be willing to help.

The woods were quiet, other than normal wildlife sounds. Those quieted as his group passed and quickly picked up again behind them. There was no way there was anyone else around other than them. They kept up a good pace, despite having to walk. His brothers were just as uneasy as he was. It was nothing he could put his finger on, but he could tell from their glances and the unusual sober looks on their faces.

Walking throughout the morning they took a quick break for lunch in the early afternoon. He called a halt when Faith began to tire, her footsteps slowing and her steps no longer steady. Crag knew they needed to take a break.

Hark broke out venison for lunch. A quick meal and a little bit of time for rest and they resumed their trek.

Rog and Hark grumbled under their breath about walking.

Fine, once we hit a place that will work to teach Faith to fly, we'll stop.

About time. Rog continued to grumble.

Good. Hark snorted. *I'm going ahead to scout out a place.* He stopped, stripped, tossed his bag to Rog and shifted. The young trees squashed to the ground and the older ones creaking but holding their own against the mass suddenly straining against them.

Was that really necessary? Crag frowned.

Hark wiggled, pulling his bulk from between the trees. He heaved upward, trying to fly. His wings pumped, creating a backlash of swirling air and pine needles. With a huge effort and possibly scraped sides, Hark lifted into the air.

Yes. I'll let you know when I find a spot. With that, he flew above the trees and away.

"Idiot." Rog swung Hark's bag over his shoulder and walked forward.

The afternoon continued much like the morning. Peaceful woods and a little bit of joking and talking back and forth. All the while Faith walked hand-in-hand with him. It made his day brighter to feel her soft, warm fingers intertwined with his. His heart warmed, seeing a peaceful smile on her face.

Faith seemed happier. Perhaps she was always meant to be a dragon. He shrugged, his thoughts circling back to his mate. There was no perhaps about it. Faith was born to be his mate.

I found a spot. You should reach it soon. I'll be there. Hark broke into his thoughts.

Is there game for supper? Crag wanted to ensure Faith wouldn't go hungry.

Don't worry, I'll have some ready. Can't let a new dragon starve!

Afternoon wound down and the woods darkened. Evening fell. Crag sniffed, the smell of cooking meat wafted across his nostrils. His stomach rumbled. They couldn't be far from the location Hark mentioned.

"We should almost be there." Crag smiled down at Faith, admiring his mate.

"Where is there?" Faith sniffed, her stomach growling along with his.

"Food, and a place to stop for the night. And enough room to teach you to fly."

"Truly?" A smile broke out across her face. "That's awesome."

"Move a little faster. I'm starving." Rog closed in on them, impatience in his tone. "Then we can fly instead of walking. Finally."

They broke through the woods into a meadow with a pond in the distance. Rog right on their tails. Crag shoved his irritation with him away. He was right. Walking everywhere was tedious. He glanced around, this would be a perfect spot to teach Faith to fly.

A fire burned merrily, meat already roasting, the source of the tempting smells.

Crag breathed deep. Beside him, Faith did the same.

"That smells so good. I'm so hungry." Her stomach growled.

His brothers grabbed a haunch of the roasting meat. Munching, stripping accompanied by Faith's gasp, and her quickly covering her eyes, they ran towards the water. Rog and Hark dove in, shifting as they entered the water, their scales gleaming from the bit of sun left.

Crag already knew how deep the river was having enjoyed it before. Faith looked longingly after his brothers as they frolicked. Then her stomach rumbled. She glanced from the fire to the water, indecision written on her face.

Crag moved up behind Faith and wrapped his arms around her. She leaned her head back on his shoulder and smiled, sliding her hands over the top of his.

"I think this is a good spot to spend the night, don't you?"

"Yes. I do." Then she giggled.

"What thoughts are running through your head?"

"This is where I first saw a dragon on the ground." Faith ducked her head, snickering. "He was in the water. It appeared he had something caught in the mud. There was lots of thrashing around going on."

CHAPTER SEVENTEEN

Faith snuck a peek at Crag from under her lashes. She laughed, his face turning scarlet.

"Oh, my God." He grabbed her, swinging her to face him. "You were here?"

"Yes." Tears came to her eyes, her belly aching from holding in her amusement. She widened her eyes, trying to stop her snickering. "Were you hurt?"

"Shut up." Crag dropped his head onto hers, growling in her ear. "You know damn well what I was doing."

Faith shivered, his breath against her ear sending tingles down her body. She couldn't wipe the smirk from her face, though. She never thought she'd see Crag blush.

"I can give you new memories." He nibbled on the lobe of her ear. He slid his hands down suggestively, caressing her curves, pulling her closer.

"Mmm. Maybe you can. I suppose I'll have to let you prove it." Faith winked. "But I'm so fond of those."

Crag rolled his eyes, grumbling. "I can't believe you saw me."

Faith giggled as he nuzzled her. He teased her with every touch. His hands following her curves, cupping the weight of her breasts in his hands. Liquid heat burrowed in her belly. Tingles erupted along the path of his fingers. She craved his hardness, aching from emptiness. She tightened her hands, digging her fingers into the muscles of his back.

Cursing, he tripped.

Faith screamed, the ground flying out from beneath them. Falling backwards, holding tight to Crag, water cascaded over their heads. The slap of the water, a shock. She choked, breathing in water. Sputtering, clawing to the top, Faith surfaced, gagging.

Crag popped up beside her. "Are you all right?"

She couldn't even breath yet, coughing, choking. She could barely tread water, let alone answer such a stupid question.

Firm arms surrounded her, supporting her. Faith melted in his arms, ignoring the dribble of water from her lips. No longer worrying about dunking under again, with Crag's support, she broke the surface. Heaving, she greedily sucked air into her aching lungs. Faith's eyes stung, tears leaked from the corners of her eyes.

"Faith, I'm so sorry." Crag's arms rubbed up and down her back. "I wasn't looking where I was going. I swear we were further from the edge."

Faith could hear the chortle of dragons. "Assholes."

"The edge gave way."

One of the two yelled. Faith had no clue which one spoke through their laughter. Assholes.

Looking down, she groaned, her dress sopping wet and darn near see through. Heading toward the bank, Faith crawled up, collapsing on the nearest patch of grass. Looking up, sucking in air, she watched Crag dive after his brothers.

Despite the dunking, Faith couldn't remember ever being so happy. The walk through the woods holding Crag's hand lit her soul with joy. The feel of his long, callused fingers intertwined with hers made her feel safe, secure, hot and bothered. Flustered, but in a totally awesome way.

Her eyes ran over Crag's body, her belly tightening with longing. Then, dragons replaced the sight of the naked men. The dragons frolicking in the water a sight to behold. Faith desperately wanted to believe Hope was as happy as she was. That Crag wasn't lying to her. Her stomach churned, please let him not be lying to her.

A slight breeze made its way across the clearing. Shivers ran up her spine. Turning, she headed to the fire. A bit of the delicious smelling venison would go down well and hopefully, the fire would dry her dress.

Sitting, the warmth from the fire warming her, removed some of the chill of her wet clothes. Turning to watch the dragons at play, Faith admired Crag rising out of the water. His dragon was magnificent. Something stirred inside her, admiring the view along with her. Faith realized it was her dragon. Happiness simmered, bubbling through her veins. A wonder, and excitement blooming. She was right where she belonged.

Crag shifted, the water cascading over him, caressing his chest and hard abdomen. He stalked gracefully toward her, the water sluicing and exposing his body to the air and her appreciative gaze.

Crag's eyes met hers, a wicked smile caressing his lips.

Looking her fill, she could see him responding to her gaze. A flush rose on her cheeks, but she refused to look away. Magnificent. Sculpted in all the right places. His cock rising at her gaze. She licked her lips, her body empty and aching to feel his touch. A proud, arrogant man she couldn't believe belonged to her.

His brothers followed behind him laughing and joking. Crag ignored them, single-mindedly heading toward her.

A blush warmed her whole body. Her nipples peaking, jutting toward him. The burning sensation of his gaze tightening her belly. The dampness of her dress doing little to hide what he did to her. She could feel her core soften, anticipating his hardness inside her. Her thighs slick with her desire.

Breathing deep, his nostrils flared, as if he could smell her arousal. He grinned, a wicked little smile that turned her insides to knots. Stepping in front of her, his desire plain for everyone to see.

Hands dragged him away. Swearing at his brothers, Crag fought to come back to her.

"It's time for dinner," Hark pointed out. "And that includes your mate. I can hear her stomach grumbling from here."

Growling, Crag sounding more like a dragon than man. "Fine. Let's eat." Turning to Faith he asked. "Is that what you want?"

"Yes, it's fine." It wasn't really. Faith eyed his bobbing cock. She wanted nothing more than to sink down on him, feeling him fill her up. Her growling stomach argued with her. It wanted food. The rest of her just wanted Crag.

"I'm going fishing." Grabbing something out of his knapsack, Hark dove in the water again. Too dark to tell what it was, Faith would assume it was something to help catch fish.

"Me, too." Rog dove in after him.

"I'll join them." Crag's gaze stoking the fire inside her. "Since I can't have what I really want yet."

Faith fanned herself. Lethal. That man was lethal.

Crag and his brothers were not gone long. Returning shortly with a net full of fish, stopping only to put on pants, they headed back toward her. They threw a couple in the fire to cook.

"Are those for you?"

"No, for you."

Faith pouted, looking at the fish tossed in the fire. Like she wanted to eat scales and bones. Cleaning them would be so much harder. Her dragon stirred inside, contradicting her. Scales and bones would keep her strong. Ick. Her dragon might like it, but in her normal skin, Faith refused to eat raw fish.

"What's wrong?"

"Usually I clean them first. I don't like eating the innards and I prefer not to eat the head."

Crag grimaced at the fire. "That's okay we'll eat those. We usually eat them in dragon form." He stared at them. "Usually raw, though."

"Ick." Faith gestured, turning toward a flat rock that was nestled close to the bank of the river. "I can clean the fish. That rock should work okay. Then I'll eat them." She shook her head, rolling her eyes. "Normally I clean them before they are cooked."

"There's more." Rog tossed a net filled with fish at her. "Feel free to go crazy."

"Of course, there is." Just like the men in her family, they expected her to cook. No, that wasn't fair. Taking a deep breath, Faith exhaled her instinctive anger. They'd been doing the cooking, making sure she was fed before they ate. They were not like her human family.

"Very good." Crag kissed her neck, sending her jumping. "We'll eat the ones in the fire already."

"Don't sneak up on me." Faith exhaled, heart pumping. She needed to stay out of her head.

Crag just laughed.

"Here." Hark walked over and dumped a bunch of chanterelles at her feet. "I found these down the river a bit, thought you might like them."

"Thank you." Aww, maybe these men weren't so bad. Faith smiled at him. "These are a wonderful addition." She poked at them. "You're sure these are chanties?"

"Yes. Crag wouldn't forgive us if we poisoned you."

Tickled pink, Faith grinned. "No, I don't suppose he would. Thank you."

"No problem. Anything for our new sister." Rog tossed an arm around Hark's shoulders, dragging him toward the fire.

Faith beamed, happiness filling her heart. They teased and taunted her but there was no meanness in it. They treated her just like they treated each other. She never wanted to lose this. She'd finally found a family that accepted her just as she was. She snorted. Not quite, they did change her into a dragon, but despite that, she belonged. Her heart knew it.

"Sometimes you just seem to know the right thing to say." Crag muttered, tossing a rock after Rog.

"And sometimes he's just an ass." Hark added. Rog growled at them. The two men began to snicker.

Faith shook her head, just like family. She couldn't wipe the smile from her face. She didn't even want to try. Scooping up the chanterelle, and wrinkling her nose at the fish, she headed to clean them.

Not soon enough, Faith put the fish and mushrooms on the rock in the fire, listening to the sizzle. She flipped them using a spatula she'd brought with. Despite the extra weight she'd brought the basics for cooking, happily anticipating being on her own. Not anticipating she would become a dragon, eating animals whole. Or practically.

She shrugged. Whatever. It all worked out.

The fish didn't take long before it was ready to eat. The aroma setting her stomach rumbling.

"Can I have your plates?" Hark and Rog handed her theirs. She put a couple of fish on each plate along with the fried chanterelle and handed them back.

Faith filled a plate Crag handed her, handing it back.

"That's for you. Eat." He kissed her head and loaded a piece of scavenged wood and sat back and ate.

She laughed to herself. Even though the brothers had obviously eaten in the river she could see them sniffing as the smell of the cooking fish tickled their noses. It was obvious they could eat more. Faith quickly finished and again filled her plate with food. The men, dragons, whatever, quickly filled their plates again.

Everyone was hungry. Spending the day out walking built up an appetite for everyone.

Faith quickly took some more fillets and put them on the rock to cook. There were plenty of chanterelles, so she added more. The aroma enticing.

Settling back, she cleaned her plate a second time. Her belly stretched, full to the brim. Rubbing it, the taste of supper lingering on her lips, Faith let out a small groan. She leaned back against a large boulder, sated to her toes.

Glancing over at Crag, her face heated, her body warming. She swallowed. He rang all her bells. Thick, muscular, handsome. Not so muscular he looked obscene. His body carried a comforting level of cushion. He wasn't fat, but he was more than muscles and bone. He made her feel delicate, feminine.

She wouldn't have gotten to know him quite so well if she met him at home. She trembled, thinking how well she knew him. The hot warmth of his flesh and the prickle of his chest hair against her hands. The feel of his muscles under his skin. A shiver ran through her, her nipples peaking. She squirmed where she sat, desire simmering in her body.

Crag glanced at her. She watched his nostrils flare and his eyes turned sultry. Her body heated. It wasn't in embarrassment, rather heat rising in her blood just from his look. Warmth blossomed between her legs. Liquid pooling, making her pussy slick. She had a feeling that under the cover of darkness she would get to know him even more. She could hardly wait.

Crag was pulling pieces from his plate tossing it up and catching it in his mouth to his brother's disgust. Faith couldn't help but chuckle.

Their antics kept everyone entertained while the fish quickly disappeared. Finished, Crag glanced over at Faith.

"Did you want to take a swim, Faith?"

"That would be refreshing, after I clean the plates." Faith looked over at Crag. "Here, give me those." She stood, grabbing the dirty plates. Looking forward to the cool water.

Crag groaned and his brothers laughed.

"What?" Faith headed to the river, hoping to cool off a bit. If Crag kept looking at her with that smolder in his eyes, she would likely tear open his pants, lift her dress and bounce on his dick until she screamed.

"I think Crag was going to steal you away for a little bit." Rog's smirk stopped when Crag smacked the back of his head.

"Oh yeah, his intentions were to fuck you hard." Hark grinned, jumping away from Crag's swing.

"Asshole."

Faith flushed crimson. Her nipples hardened, and her juices ran down her leg.

"Oh." She looked at Crag. "I'm sorry. I didn't even think. I just wanted to get the dishes done. You know, so it wouldn't be so hard to clean them in the morning."

"Don't worry about it. We have the rest of the night." He shot her a crooked grin while his eyes simmered with lust. It thrilled her to her toes.

Faith set the dishes on the bank and waded in chest deep, raising her dress to keep it dry. Faith pulled it off and flung it to the shore. The cool water was not cooling her heated blood a bit. Glancing at the shore another wave of desire washed through her. The sky darkened enough so that the only light to be seen was the fire.

Crag was standing up, looking her way. His silhouette highlighted by the fire. The intensity radiating from him caught her breath.

His brothers, talking and joking, never seeming to be at a loss for words. The sky darkened, shrouding even Crag's features from view. Faith slowly started rising out of the water. She could wash the plates without her nudity being seen.

Crag stilled. Faith could feel his attention centered on her.

Her breathing hitched. She wanted his arms around her. His hardness penetrating her. His firm body surrounding hers. Her pussy on fire, her breathing labored, Faith stepped closer, the water lapping at her breasts, her belly, and then pussy as she drew closer to the bank.

Crag jumped up, lunging toward her.

Suddenly, talons snatched her into the air. Faith screamed. The wind lashing against her naked form, goosebumps rising across her body. Higher and higher, she shivered continually while caught in the grasp of a strange dragon.

"Crag! Help me!" The words torn from her throat were lost in the wind. Tears formed in her eyes. "Let me go!" Too afraid to struggle, Faith huddled close to the only warmth, the talons of the beast that stole her away.

Faith shivered from the roar of rage below. Even though she was scared, Faith felt nothing but pity for her kidnapper. Crag would show no mercy when he caught them.

CHAPTER EIGHTEEN

Crag was listening to Hark and Rog exchange barbs when he saw a shadow loom over Faith, followed by her scream. He let out a roar. Faith was being carried away in the talons of a dragon, surrounded by a dozen or more white dragons.

White dragons, it has to be Blanc. Growling, fire shooting from his snout, Crag sprung up, changing, leaping after them.

Ari! My mate has been taken!

Rog and Hark followed behind. The white dragons flew fast. Faster than he'd expected. He couldn't imagine how frightened Faith was. The evening had been so peaceful, lulling him into complacency. Why the hell had he dropped his guard? His worst fears came to life.

I'm on my way with Hope.

Crag thought of all the things that could happen to Faith. If she thought about it, she could change, but she didn't know how to fly. She might learn by being dropped, but she could easily plummet to her death instead. He should've called in reinforcements right away. He was uneasy from the get-go when he found out Blanc had left.

Following them, and never quite catching up, infuriated him. Expressing his displeasure for all to hear, Crag roared. His wings ached from the cold, and the extra effort of racing to catch the ice dragons. Anger swirled. He would destroy Blanc. Render him limb from limb. No one stole his mate.

He could see the dragons up ahead. They were fast, pulling ahead the longer they flew. Crag kept them in his sight, though just barely. They had his mate. He would follow her to the ends of the earth.

Pain shot through his chest, his heart breaking open. He loved her. Faith. His mate. His future. He would do anything for her. Once he'd rescued her, if she truly wanted to stay with her family, he would find some way to be okay with it. It wouldn't be easy. Fitting in with humans. He would, though, for her.

Crag worried they didn't send some of the dragons back to delay them. There were enough of them to take on him and his brothers. The ice dragons appear to be smaller in stature but there were enough of them to do some serious damage. And they were fast.

Crag flew, trying to keep them in sight. It got darker and darker. His vision and their gleaming white scales in the moonlight kept him on track. He wondered if there were planning on stopping for the night.

He ground his teeth, wanting to paint the sky in flames. He should have taught her to fly. He should have taught her how to speak telepathically to him. His chest rumbled. Regrets sucked. He needed his mate, and he needed her safe.

He continued to fly, ignoring his brothers behind him. Knowing they had his back.

From the feel of the silent night around him, the circadian rhythm of the evening insects, and the nocturnal animals waking up, it was getting late. He was high enough not to stop the rhythm of the night.

The night air turned frigid. This high up, with no clothing Faith had to be freezing. She could die from hypothermia if she didn't reach warmth soon. The thought of this happening to Faith had his blood burning through his veins. His eyes narrowed as he studied the dragons in front of him. With a burst of speed brought on by the adrenaline coursing through his body at the thought of harm coming to his mate, he lessened the distance.

His only thought was to rescue Faith. Hopefully the dragon inside her kept her warmer than a normal human.

Finally, he could see the ice dragons slow. They were glancing back, seeing if he was still there. His dark scales and the first lid on his eye covering their glow, he knew he had to be nearly invisible to their eyes. One thing a fire dragon could do was hide, especially in the dark.

He could tell his brothers flew behind him still. They would never miss a chance for mischief, nor would they miss a chance to save family. This was a chance for both.

The ice dragons swooped down and disappeared. Crag and his brothers burst forward putting on extra speed, aiming for the same location the dragons had disappeared. They circled the mountain. They must have gone in. Crag could not see an entrance, but he knew it was there.

Hark check the snow line see if there are any prints to show where they entered. Rog, checked the edge of the tree line see if you can find a way in. I'll take the center section and do the same.

Okay, will do. Rog headed toward the trees, flying low over the tops.

You can count on me, bro. Hark flew, hovering over the snow. Crag knew Hark was their best tracker. The trace of a tail, the faintest impression of a talon and he would have them.

Crag sped to his area to search. His gut told him he would find Faith. Blanc better just hope she wasn't harmed.

Crag knew they had gone inside the mountain somehow. It was just a matter of finding it. They were too far back to have seen exactly where they had gone in. Unfortunately, it was time he did not want to waste. He flew quietly. He didn't want to give away his position. Caves could go for miles and he wanted Faith back as soon as possible.

Anything?

Not yet.

No.

Keep searching. He knew he didn't have to tell them that but he couldn't help it. From the lack of snarky replies, they were just as worried.

No matter how much he and his brothers and sisters like to tease each other when it came to what mattered they stuck together. Time flew by. Each possible cavern searched with no clue to the entrance. Anger warred with despair. What were they doing with his mate?

Hearing wings Crag looked up, hoping he could see the dragons leaving, but it was only his brother Ari, Ari's mate and his sisters come to help.

What are you doing? Crag could see Ari hovering above him as he looked down.

We're searching for an entrance. We were too far away to see where they had gone in, so now we have to search for it. Crag looked around at his siblings. *How did you get here so quickly?*

We were flying to help Ari move Hope's family to his weyr. Juevatorj chimed in.

Yes, we were exploring. Belissa glanced at Jeuvatorj. *Someone has been flirting and we followed him north. We could tell we were close when you called to Ari, so came to help.*

I wasn't flirting!

Belissa chuckled. *Of course not.*

Ari frowned at his sisters. *We'll talk about that later.*

Belissa laughed while Jeuvatorj rolled her eyes.

Evidently, we were farther north than I realized. Hope was flying and I was following behind her. I thought it best to leave her family for a bit, so she's been practicing. Ari glanced around.

Crag shook his head; glad they were all so close to help get his mate back.

We'll help. It should cut the time in half. What do you want us to do? Ari asked.

Crag explained where they'd searched and the pattern they were using. They couldn't chance missing the smallest opening.

Belisa and Juevatorj headed to Hark and Rog and quickly split the territory. Hope hadn't yet mastered mind speak so Ari was telling her what was said. They too split off to search. Crag knew it wouldn't be long now before they found the entrance.

After what seemed like hours Hark trumpeted. He had found the entrance to the caverns. They all converged on the opening. They had found no other exit. That didn't mean there wasn't one, but chances were the ice dragons were inside.

Rog, stand guard on the exit. Make sure no one gets past.

I will.

They had no idea what the ice dragons had planned. Crag didn't know if this was a temporary weyr or not. For all he knew, everything that spilled from Blanc's mouth were lies. The only way they would find out was to go in.

Crag went in first, arrowing through the entrance. Hark and Ari followed. The females took up the rear. He knew better than to suggest one of his sisters stand guard. They would bite the first thing that came through before they checked to see who it was. No way did Crag or his brothers want the female's poison coursing through their body.

When they wanted, a dragoness could change the chemicals in their bite. Depending on what they bit, it could be lethal. Luckily for him and his brothers, they were mostly immune, having been bitten often as children as they fought and played.

In a situation like this, their bite would be lethal. Their reaction time was fast, faster than the larger, male dragons. Sometimes his sisters lacked the common sense to check who they bit before they did it. Crag didn't want to be on the end of a bite if they needed a fast getaway.

Hope was too new a dragon to put her on guard duty. And with Faith being her sister, she wanted to be in on the action. With Ari there, Crag wouldn't have to worry about her.

The entrance led straight into a tunnel, not an open cave like they were used to. Perhaps this was not the only entrance. They had seen no sign of another but that didn't mean anything in the cave system. It could come out on another side of the mountain.

Crag didn't know what he would do if they could find no trace of them. But he knew he would not stop hunting.

They silently flew through the tunnels. Running on the stone would have their talons clicking, alerting the ice dragons they were coming. Flying, Crag hoped the swish of their wings would go unnoticed.

If the ice dragons were going through the tunnel, they probably thought that they had escaped successfully and were not keeping silent. The air in these tunnels was cold, colder than their weyr. He wasn't surprised. The ice dragons would prefer the cold where the fire dragons needed the heat from the underground volcanoes to keep them warm.

He thought all dragons needed some heat, if only for hatching. Perhaps he was wrong. The chill of the air sent a shiver down his spine. He could only imagine how cold Faith was.

If this was only a temporary weyr, then it meant nothing more than a convenient hiding spot. He still didn't hear anything.

Do you hear anything?

No, nothing yet. Ari was the first to answer.

Hark? Do you hear anything?

There is a faint noise up ahead. I'm not sure what it is though.

We have to be very quiet then. I don't want them escaping with Faith again.

We will not let you down, brother. Ari's solemn words struck home. First hatched, he led the rest, speaking for them all.

All his siblings chimed in agreement. Crag knew they would not let him down. Ari didn't need to put that into words, but it was still good to hear. They flew as quiet as they could, single file due to the lack of space in the tunnel. Crag glimpsed an opening ahead on the right. The tunnel still continued forward but they had to be careful. He slowed hoping the back breeze did not alert anyone inside. If anyone was inside.

He slowly eased to the entrance. At first glance he saw an empty cave. He went to pass when he frowned and entered the cave.

Don't follow me. I need to see something.

He checked quickly, none of his siblings followed. He could never be sure whether they would listen or not. He flew in, listening carefully. No one was here. To see better in the darkness, he shot flame to light the room. He reeled back in shock.

The floor of what was obviously a nest was covered in eggs. He didn't know how long they had been there. The hatchlings inside had died without a fighting chance of life. His flames had reflected through the thin shells and showed the lifeless bodies. It appeared that only two had made it out of the shell.

He hovered over the eggs, sorrow arrowing through him at the loss of life. His heart clenched. The floor of the nest was cold. There was no way these hatchlings could've hatched on their own. It was obvious from the way it was set up that the ice dragons did indeed need heat to hatch. From the evidence of just this one room, this was their weyr. They would have to search carefully. He quietly slid back into the tunnel and rejoined his siblings.

What was there?

What made you so sad?

It was hatchlings. A whole nest and it looks like only two cracked shell. The nest was cold as ice.

He swallowed back the ache in his throat. He could feel the sorrow emanating from his siblings. The loss of hatchlings a tragedy, no matter the race of the dragon.

Perhaps there is more to this than meets the eye. I wonder if they have a reason for kidnapping Faith. Ari spoke.

Crag nodded his head stiffly. *It still does not excuse the fact that they did it.*

His brother should know that Crag could not easily forgive the theft of his mate. The woman whom he discovered held his heart in her tiny, ornery hands. He grinned. She would argue the fact, but that would only prove it.

No. But maybe it is not cause for a death sentence.

He hated when Ari was the voice of reason. *We will see.* He couldn't help the fact that he sounded grumpy. Passing a couple more chambers, filled with more unhatched eggs, Crag was beginning to believe there existed a reason for the kidnapping. Something more than just desiring a mate.

They continued on. Similar to their weyr, it appeared that families had different wings. Each with its own nest in the central living area. It was evident at one point this weyr held a huge population of dragons. He could feel the sorrow emanating from his family. They were heartbroken at the loss of life.

Crag could admit to confusion. He could not understand why Faith was stolen. Something didn't add up. He wondered how much of Blanc's story was true. There was no evidence of dragons still living here. He saw no way they could when it appeared that the volcano from the mountain was no longer living.

They progressed further in and Crag realized perhaps it wasn't totally dead. The deeper they went, the warmer it became. It didn't have enough warmth to hatch the eggs they had seen, but perhaps it bore enough warmth to keep those hardy enough to hatch, alive. He realized at this point there was no need to keep Rog on guard. Crag called him to follow.

Why don't you join us? Just follow the tunnel straight in. Be quiet, but you don't have to be too quiet as all the caverns we passed were empty.

Will do. It's been quiet out here. No activity at all.

Crag was relieved at his reassurance. He hadn't realized how much he worried about them taking Faith back out. Even if they hadn't passed them. They flew deeper into the mountain. If Crag was not mistaken, they were deep as the mountain was tall. Still they had not located them.

Crag tried to stop worrying. He could hear activity up ahead, feel the warmth. Not as warm as he preferred, though enough to at least keep Faith dying from the cold.

The noise ahead was a sharp contrast to the silence of the rooms they passed. The ice dragons must have been sure they would not have followed them in. They would find out they were wrong.

Crag wondered how old exactly these dragons were. Blanc looked like an adult but he appeared to be younger than Crag and his siblings. It was obvious Blanc wasn't mated since he had participated in Crag's own ritual. No mated dragons would even feel the pull.

It still made no sense why they stole Faith. They flew, continuing down toward the activity. The air warming and the darkness lightening. The noise grew louder. They slowed, approaching what appeared to be a large cavern. Larger than all the ones they passed.

Crag lowered himself to the ground and shifted forms, not wanting to be seen. His siblings followed his lead landing quietly behind him. He crept forward, inching further into the large room. He maneuvered until he was behind two stalagmites. He slowly stood.

From the corner of his eye he could see his siblings do the same. Ari and Hope huddling together. They peered into the room.

Faith was in the center of the room, having changed into her dragon at some point. Crag knew, without a doubt, it was her. While white like the dragons surrounding her, her shimmering scales gave evidence of the fire inside her. She was looking around and making little chirps, much like the sound his dam made to them. Surrounding her were hatchlings, maybe three dozen, snuggling close. A couple of older ones stood a bit further away, looking yearningly toward Faith.

A few human women huddled off to the side. Crag wondered where they had all come from. Probably kidnap victims as much as Faith, he was sure. They watched the dragons in fear, flinching when any of them noticed them.

He wondered why they were there. Only a couple of the dragons looked old enough to be Blanc. Crag was not familiar enough with him that he could pick him out.

Looking around, his stomach sank. None of the dragons were adults. Each one was a hatchling and none of them looked healthy. They were crowding around Faith seeking comfort. It appeared that Blanc's story was true, but it hadn't told the whole truth. These hatchlings were freezing, huddled together in the last bit of warmth in this dying volcano.

Crag watched them in sorrow, not knowing quite what to do. He heard more chirping and realized his sisters had been unable to resist the crying of the hatchlings. Back in their dragons, they joined Faith in the center, where most of the warmth emanated. Cuddling around the hatchlings, they tried to comfort them and keep them warm. He watched Hope pull from Ari's hand. She too changed and joined the rest of the females.

I think they need us all. Ari's voice sounded as sorrowful as he felt.

Do you think we will be able to save them? Crag cleared his throat. Born into tragic circumstances, Crag could forgive Blanc. He obviously was trying to save them all.

I will call our Sire. He can alert the elders so that perhaps the few ice dragons left can survive.

For once Rog was silent. Not even he was able to muster up a joke when faced with these hatchlings. He was the first male to change and go forward. Sweeping the stragglers and the oldest dragons, toward the center to keep them huddled on the tiny bit of warmth from the dying volcano.

They all shifted and went forward to try to protect the young as best they could. Crag knew there was no hope for those that hadn't hatched. He couldn't imagine the sorrow they felt. They might be too young though. Survival being their main thought. Warmth and food. Looking around, Crag realized they needed food. Lots of it.

Hark, can you hunt? We are going to need food if they are to survive. Crag swung his head to Ari next.

Can you get the women out of here? It's obvious they are human.

Good idea. We don't want any of them to become prey. I'll help Hark hunt. We will need a lot of food. Ari changed, walking up to the frightened women.

"You came. We weren't sure you would." Blanc sidled up next to Crag. Only at that point did he realize how young Blanc really was. His dragon was a quarter of the size of Crag's. "Only a couple of us were old enough to remember about the mating bond."

"Is that why you took my mate? To get us to come here?" Crag's heart bled knowing the hopelessness these hatchlings were facing. "What happened here?"

Blanc shook his head, his eyes whirling with agitation. "I don't know. I was one of the few dragons that hatched when there were still adults here. They all died, leaving us alone." His voice broke, twisting Crag's gut.

The pain in his voice made Crag want to make it better. Damn it. He couldn't help but admire the spunk Blanc displayed in stealing his mate to try to save his race.

"We will not." Crag's voice caught.

The phrase echoed by all of the adults in the room. In that instance he realized that it wasn't just the mating bond that created adults. Sometimes life stepped in as it had in this moment, creating that crystal-clear epiphany that moved you away from childhood, sending you forward with no desire to look back.

Ari, we have room.

Yes, we do.

Blanc looked around and back at Crag. Hope brimming in his eyes. Crag could no more take revenge for him stealing Faith and bringing her here than he could reject him now. Crag crowded Blanc sweeping him toward the rest of the hatchlings, offering comfort. Blanc settled down happily at the unspoken acknowledgment. The relief unmistakable on his features as he did so.

Crag could hear Hark contacting their Sire. He and his siblings continued to huddle the hatchlings together for warmth. He looked around and caught Ari's eye.

How many do you think will want to stay with us?

He could hear Ari's laugh. *Do you see Hope and Faith? We might as well count on all of them.*

What about our sisters? Will they want any?

He looked at them and realized that really wasn't an option. The real comfort was coming from Faith and

Hope. The hatchlings seem drawn to them. Crag looked at them. Both of them so recently turned. He realized they had become the women they were meant to be. The dragons they were meant to be. And with both of them gravid from the mating ritual their maternal instinct kicked in.

Crag smirked. He was sure Faith hadn't a clue. That would be an interesting discussion.

They are wonderful. He hadn't realized that he had spoken that for all his siblings to hear, but from the laughter he had.

They certainly are.

If Ari could agree Crag had no reason to be embarrassed at his sentiment. Faith was everything he'd hoped for in a mate and more. Now he just had to ensure that she realized it. Eyeing the hatchlings around the room, Crag smiled. Now he even had more ammunition to persuade her to stay.

CHAPTER NINETEEN

Faith stood surrounded by baby dragons. She couldn't help but try to comfort them. Something inside her demanded it. She shifted trying to escape her kidnappers. She began plummeting, her weight tearing her from the claws of the dragon that had taken her away. Before she could hit the ground, she was surrounded by the dragons lifting her up and carrying her forward.

Each time she had tried to flap her wings to fly she slid, spiraling uncontrollably. Each time saved by the dragons that were taking her away. She could feel the separation from her mate the further apart they took her from Crag. In that moment Faith realized that it was not freedom she wanted. Her heart swelled. It was freedom to be herself and Crag gave her that.

She realized she loved him. When she thought she would never see him again, sorrow filled her. Then her heart broke when she saw the baby dragons starving and freezing. With no questions asked, Faith stepped forward to comfort them.

Looking at those that brought her here, she realized why. She knew they couldn't continue to survive on their own.

She could only hope from the roar that Crag let loose as she was taken away that he followed her. Not to the ends of the earth, just here, where he was needed by her and the little ones.

Surrounded by the little dragons, Faith realized Crag arrived. It thrummed through her blood. Her heart responded to the beat of his. The air itself took on a different quality when he was near, that's how she knew. Knew they were bonded to their souls. She believed somehow, he would save them all.

She looked up from comforting the dragons and watched as more dragons converged on the babies. More female dragons, and one by one they came and offered comfort. Her heart glowed with pride when she saw Crag talking to the young dragon that stole her away.

The look on his face was heartbreaking. She knew the baby dragons need for comfort and love, but Crag knew something more. When he stepped forward, taking the young dragon that had stolen her under his wing, her heart burst with love. He was a good man, and he was hers.

Looking up, catching Crag's eye, had her pulse fluttering. Her heart swelled, filling with happiness. She knew somehow this would all work out. The little dragons would be saved and she was determined to keep Crag for her own. Her body crying for his and her soul reached out, wanting nothing more than to be entwined in his limbs.

After a while, with all the adults surrounding them, the little ones settled down and slept. Faith watched Crag and his siblings and realized they appeared to be communicating. Faith wondered how they did it. She studied them and tried concentrating but she was unable to hear them. Faith wondered what their names were but she didn't want to disturb the little dragons snuggled against her now they'd gone to sleep.

Faith looked around and realized that the cavern was cold. The warmth underneath her feet couldn't make up for the chill in the air. She wasn't alone. She watched the baby dragons shiver as if one. They needed to get these little ones somewhere warmer. Faith had no idea where they could take them, or if they could even travel.

She noticed the other dragons perking up and looking toward one of the tunnels. She looked that way also, wondering what they were waiting for. She didn't have to wonder long. In flew a flock of dragons, one after the other, circling the little ones. Faith wasn't quite sure that she liked being circled, especially since she was in the center of all the dragons.

Faith also wasn't sure using flock was correct, but she had no idea of what dragons call themselves. Birds would be a flock and they were flying so she would go with that. Still more dragons flew in but with these they appeared to be carrying livestock. Actually, now that Faith looked, she could see that they were deer and other small critters that the little dragons would be able to eat.

The noise woke the little ones. They saw the food arrive, flooding the air with excitement. She wondered how long it had been since they had eaten. She didn't think there were enough of the bigger dragons to keep all of them fed properly. And she was right from the way they fell on the food. Dragons kept bringing more, until every little dragon had food. Her eyes swelled, tears brimming her eyes, aching over their situation.

Faith made her way over to Crag, smiling at the contented crunching going on around her. A deep sense of satisfaction swamped her as she looked and saw each of the little dragons eating, as if they were her own.

"Are you okay?" Crag nuzzled her neck, running his face along hers.

"I'm fine. Where did all these dragons come from?" She breathed deeply, his scent burrowing deep in her lungs.

"They're my family. They're from my weyr." Crag looked around and Faith could see the sense of satisfaction on his face. "We told them that these hatchlings needed help or they would die. We could not let a whole species of dragons perish."

"So, hatchlings are what you call baby dragons?"

"Yes, and the older ones would be younglings. But they've had the responsibility of adults so that may not be appropriate either." Crag wrapped his neck around hers. His wings pulled her in tight.

Unconsciously Faith started matching his actions wrapping her face and neck around his body, just as he was doing to her.

"How big is the flock that flew in?" She had to keep her mind on the questions she wanted to ask. Since she was determined to stay with Crag, she had to learn. She wanted him to know that she could learn so that he would keep her.

"Flock?" Crag's laughter boomed around the cavern. Some of the little ones looked up and then went back chewing and crunching.

Faith head butted him at his response. Ass.

"It's called a flight of dragons. Our particular group of dragons is a clan and we live in a weyr. Why would you call us flock?"

Faith shrugged. "Because they flew in like a flock of birds. I didn't know what else they would be called."

Crag smiled at her and rubbed his head against hers. Faith liked how it felt, his scales rubbing up against hers. His body was big, big and warm against hers. She sniffed. Faith realized she could smell a spicy scent emanating from Crag.

She crowded closer to him. Mmm, he smelled good. Faith wiggled trying to get as close to him as she could. Her pulse raced and her breath coming faster. Faith stirred her tail around behind her. Her body started heating as Crag's tail wrapped around hers. Faith shifted closer. Her body tingling and her scales sensitive to Crag's every touch.

Their combined scents were driving her little wild. Crag started pulling her under him when he froze at the sound of a woman's voice.

"Oh, no, you don't. There are hatchlings here."

Faith slid her head under Crag's neck and looked at where the voice was coming from. A coal black dragon stood there glaring at Crag. Faith quickly ducked her head back and hid her face in his side.

"You don't have to worry about me. He knows better." Faith could hear nails clicking on the ground, coming closer. She kept her head buried in his side, breathing his scent into her lungs. "Look at me." Faith couldn't resist the command in the soft-spoken words.

She looked up into the eyes of the dragon and realized that this must be Crag's mother. He had her same golden eyes. She was not near the size of him, but she was bigger than Faith. Faith was beginning to think she was a runt. All but one of the adult dragons were much larger than her.

"Hello." Faith had no idea of what to say. How do you greet the mother of the dragon you were determined to keep?

"Well aren't you a tiny thing? Move away from my son, I want to look at you." Faith didn't budge. She felt Crag's head bump her away and glared at him.

"Go ahead, my dam won't hurt you." He pushed her closer to his mother again, his *dam*. Faith could hear her laugh and switched her glare to her.

"Oh, I'm not laughing at you. I'm laughing at my son. It's evident he didn't get a nice, biddable mate. I couldn't be happier." Faith heard Crag growl. Faith jumped back in surprise as his dam swung around and swatted him with her tail.

She giggled. His mother smiled at her, while Crag grumbled.

"You just have to learn how to handle him. Now, what's your name?"

"I'm Faith Albright."

"Nice to meet you Faith Albright. Welcome to the clan." She looked around. "Now I need to meet my other son's mate." She turned and started lumbering away. "Ari, where's your mate? Hope, right?"

Faith couldn't help but laugh as another dragon jumped and looked toward his mother. That was one of Crag's siblings she hadn't met. Then, her words sunk in. She turned towards Crag. He came close to her again, entwined his neck with hers, and pulled her in against his side with his wing.

"Would you like to explore a little bit?"

"Where's Hope? Your dam called her Ari's mate?" His question didn't register. She'd been following after Hope wanting to save her from the dragons. Perhaps they weren't what she thought, but a niggling worry stuck in her mind. Now she could see for herself.

"See, the little copper dragon? That's Hope."

"Truly? She's beautiful."

"Yes." Crag nodded. "I wouldn't lie to you."

Faith craned her neck, watching Hope. Even as a dragon, Faith could tell that was her sister. She couldn't explain it, she just knew. Crag's brother, the one she

237

hadn't met, nuzzled her sister's neck, twining his head with hers.

Hope rubbed her snout against his, body wiggling. That was her sister, scales and all. Hope never could sit still. Faith imagined she gave the large, solemn looking dragon a run for his money.

Her whole body relaxed. Hope appeared happy. Joy oozing from her scales. Flicking her tongue out, Faith swore she could taste it. Exhaling, contentment filling her, she turned to Crag.

"Thank you." She nuzzled Crag, enjoying his spicy scent. She turned and glided toward Hope. "Hope." She nuzzled her sister's jaw. "I was so worried."

"About what?" Hope pulled from the larger dragon, focusing on her. "Why would you worry? You are the one we were looking for."

"I saw the dragon grab you and fly away. I followed, determined to get you back."

Hope laughed. "Is that why I followed you? You left before me."

Faith squirmed. "Well, I wanted an adventure, something more than we had at home."

"And have you found that?" Hope arched a large brow.

Faith had no idea a dragon's face could be so expressive. She glanced at Crag, impatiently swishing his tail, watching her. "I believe I have."

Hope slapped her tail against Faith's flank, "Then get back to it."

Faith grinned, nuzzled Hope and headed back to Crag. Her adventure. Her sister safe and happy and both of their lives turned crazy in a fantasy come to life. Entwining her neck with Crag's, Faith sighed, filled with happiness.

"So, want to go exploring?"

Faith nodded eagerly. Her senses whirling from his closeness.

Faith followed him down the tunnel. She realized that her eyes were adjusting to the light level. Even though it was dark, she could see. That was cool. She hadn't had time to get used to her dragon. She couldn't wait to learn to fly. There was an awful lot about this body that she needed to learn. Faith wondered if she'd ever get used to it.

Crag's tail swished across the ground in front of her as he walked. Faith's eyes kept coming back to it. She watched it, and her insides grew warm. She admired the spikes that grew from the back of his spine, deadly yet they drew her eye. She could see the tips of his horns on his head as he walked. Faith wanted to run her tongue over them. She giggled realizing her dragon was turned on.

Crag peeked back over his shoulder, his eyes questioning.

"Nothing." She swatted his tail with her arm, leg, whatever.

It seemed that in her dragon form that everything about Crag attracted her. He seemed mighty, like he could conquer anyone that threatened her, and that thrilled her. It was a primitive reaction that sent longing through her. His scent called to her, hot and spicy, tempting her.

He turned around, leading her away from the hatchlings. She glanced at Crag and back at the little ones disappearing from view.

Faith moved in closer and nipped him.

Crag's head swung around, the heat in them making his eyes glow. "They will be all right. No one will harm them."

He turned somehow in the impossibly small tunnel and crowded her into an opening she hadn't noticed. The intensity in his eyes and a sharp increase in his spicy scent had her nostrils flaring. Faith could feel her nails sharpen. Her belly tightened. Her claws opened and closed on the ground in anticipation.

The dragon stalked her, driving her backwards. Her sight sharpened and all her senses seemed alive. Faith didn't feel like prey. She felt glorious ready to take on the male dragon. Anticipation bubbled in her blood. He would have to earn the right to mount her.

She stopped in the middle of the room. It just seemed the right place to do so. Crag tried forcing Faith into the corner but she stood her ground, nipping at him. His dragon scales gleamed in the darkened cave. The slightest tint of green in his scales appeared to glisten in the darkness. His spikes running down his back flared, seeming larger than normal. It sent a thrill down her back.

Heat ran through her veins. Her scent swirled in the air, a tease and a challenge. Crag's scent changed. It deepened, becoming darker, appealing to her senses. Arousal slid through her. His eyes gleamed, daring her to take what she wanted.

Faith rumbled, deep from her belly. Crouching down, she waited then pounced.

Challenge accepted.

CHAPTER TWENTY

With a snicker, Crag slid to the side. He wouldn't make this easy on her. He stalked towards Faith, arousal running through his veins. Faith seemed to instinctively know how to challenge his dragon. His scales gleamed, his spikes flaring for the dance. The beginning of the mating dance that would complete them and tie them together for life.

He hadn't pushed. Faith was new to his world. He knew it would happen in time. Fate declared her his. But she had initiated the ritual instinctively and he would not turn back or ignore the challenge.

No male dragon would. He could scent her arousal and her excitement mixed with the subtle thread of challenge. Her eyes glowed a beautiful blue. The copper base of her scales seemed to be lit with fire, making the white translucent and the tips glow as blue as her eyes. She was magnificent, opalescent. She was his.

He smirked knowing Faith would object. He didn't care. Looking at her, tasting her passion in the

243

air, he would never give her up. He stalked towards her. His nails grew in preparation for holding the female down. No female dragon worth her salt would calmly accept his possession. They would possess each other. A battle for the ages. Crag snorted. Seeing the gleam in Faith's eyes, he knew she wouldn't make it easy. A thrill snaked down his back for the coming ritual, raising and lowering his spikes, showing them off like a peacock.

He feinted right and she spun still facing him. He feinted to the left and again she countered his move. He could feel himself harden the softer scales on his belly protecting him from the ground. He knew from her scent that she was softening, preparing to accept him.

He feinted again to the left. She didn't know what he was planning. He hopped as she swung her tail at him. He spun to the right. She again followed his movement. He feinted to the left and quickly to the right again. She spun, slipping sideways. Her tail giving him the opportunity he needed. In the split second before she corrected her movement, he pounced.

Crag mounted her. He held Faith in place with his larger body. Claws dug into the ground, holding her so that she could not get away. She twisted her head and bit him in the neck. Her fore claws dug into his front legs. His jaws clamped around her neck, holding her in place. She raised her back end to try to buck him off and he slid home. Faith stilled, her claws drawing blood. He hissed. His chest pressed hers to the ground, leaving her vulnerable and filled with his cock.

Faith moved trying to buck him off. He moved and slammed home again. Her claws stretched and grabbed. Now she was holding onto him rather than trying to tear him off. He again pulled back and she raised her haunches trying to keep him inside her. Crag slid home again and he could feel her tighten on him, holding him to her.

He rocked, enjoying the tight grasp of her muscles. Crag groaned, his cock encased in her tight heat. His tip expanded, sliding into her silken glory. He rocked faster, sliding his erection in and out of her sensitive passage.

Faith growled, tightening on him. She spasmed around him, trying to milk him of his seed.

Crag shifted, his back legs locking hers into place. He slammed home again and again. She tried to wiggle underneath him then realized she was at his mercy. The flash of heat around his penis and the sudden drenching of her passage proved her excitement. The shiver that ran through her body in silent surrender as she convulsed around him, set him off. He held her still as he slammed into her in a staccato rhythm.

In and out, in and out, his thickness forcing its way through the tight softness of her pussy. He rammed one last time into her and held still, his penis engorged then exploding as she roared and tightened on him. Her whole body shook. With each clench of her muscles on him, he ejaculated into her. The mix of their fluids coated her insides and the heat they generated melded them, saturating their bodies and changing and matching their scents.

Crag held on. He could not disengage until the mating was done. He was locked inside of her until they were one. Faiths legs slid out from under her, dropping her to the ground and dragging him with her.

"Oh, my God." Faith's voice held wonder and exhaustion. "I can still feel you inside me, throbbing."

"When our scents have changed our mating is completed." Crag nuzzled her neck. He shifted, putting more weight on his legs. She was so much tinier than him, physically at any rate, and he didn't want to crush her. Personality wise, and stubbornness, she was his match.

"I thought we had completed the mating ritual." She rubbed her head against him. Crag was enjoying the swirling scents that were winding through them and releasing as their scales slid against each other. The slight disturbances were sending out their combined pheromones. Alerting all in the area that their mating was complete.

"We had completed the portion changing you into a dragon. Our dragons still had to mate to complete the change in our scents to show everyone that you are mine." He could see her start to bristle but it was a faint effort. Definitely for show. He could smell her satisfaction. "And, that I am yours."

She relaxed under him, twisting to flick him with her tongue. He stretched, letting her groom him. The pheromones in the air settled down and Crag could feel himself shrink. He shifted and pulled free, relaxing next her. He pulled her in close, his wings gathering her tight to him.

We are one now.

Oh, my God. I knew you were talking to your family before. I just couldn't figure out how.

Crag chuckled. Faith was definitely smarter than he had given her credit for.

Oh, you did, did you? We have to have a special bond, either blood or be mated to be able to mind speak. We can also talk to anyone mated to those of our blood.

That definitely would be convenient. Can the other dragons hear you?

Which ones are you referring to? The ice dragons? No. They are not related to us.

Can everyone hear us now?

No. Mates have a special bond, a direct line to speak to each other.

Faith settled quietly. Crag was beginning to get a little worried. He figured she needed to think it through though, so he didn't want to interrupt.

That is so awesome.

You don't mind then? Crag could feel the happiness spreading inside him. He wasn't going to start singing and dancing in joy but he could feel the lightness inside his soul. The soul entwined with Faith's.

Crag moved, wrapping himself around her. He could completely encircle her, content to stay like this. Surrounding Faith and keeping her all to himself. A slight shiver ran through Faith.

Are you cold? The room they were in was chilled. It brought back to mind the problem they were facing. *We have to remove the hatchlings from this weyr. They will die with no heat and no adults to teach them to hunt. This whole weyr reeks of death and despair. Until we know what killed the adult ice dragons, the hatchlings are at risk.*

Where will we take them?

I would take them to our weyr. My brother Ari and I have been preparing our own place for the last couple of centuries. It is warm, wrapped as it is around a new volcano. The whole mountain chain that houses the clan is active. A perfect nest for the hatchlings.

How will you take them there?

Enough adults have come to help that we should be able to carry them if they are still too young to fly.

Crag nuzzled her. *We know that some of them know how to fly already.*

Faith laughed, her joy apparent.

CHAPTER TWENTY-ONE

Crag's warmth surrounded her, something she needed in this chilled room. She thought about all that had happened and then realized that though he had said that they were mated, he had not made any mention of her going with him. He had only talked about the hatchlings.

So, you will take them to your home?

Yes, Ari and I will take them to our home. Crag wrapped his neck around hers brushing his muzzle against her head. *First, I will take you home since you haven't yet learned to fly.*

Faith froze. She had thought that as they were mated, she would go with him. She dropped her head to the ground, suppressing the hurt she felt. She refused to let it show. Faith hoped against hope that Crag would be keeping her with him. But now he had said he was taking her home.

Despair flooded her veins. She tightened her eyelids determined to keep the tears from falling. The tears she could feel gathering, achingly at the back of

251

her eyes. She swallowed and mentally braced herself. She would not let him know how much she was hurting.

Do you want to explore more of this weyr? Or did you want to start shuttling the hatchlings as soon as possible? Even her voice in her head sounded choked up.

Crag looked at her. Faith could see the questions in his eye. She nuzzled his neck. She couldn't seem to help herself. He relaxed against her. Surely, she read him wrong. She closed her eyes, trying to keep the tears inside. He wouldn't change her just to abandon her.

I would like to stay here forever, as long as I had you next to me. Crag sighed. *But we need to start getting the little ones out of here if they are to survive.*

Faith nodded and stood, watching Crag lumber to his feet. Faith realized how large he truly was when he reached his complete height. She sidled up next to him, looking up. Way up. He stood twice as tall as her. She glanced behind them, still comparing their bodies. Every way she looked, he was twice as big as her. Her tail gave her some length but he dwarfed her. Her torso fit easily between his forelegs and his back legs.

Heat flooded her body and face when she realized exactly how she knew she fit between them. It ought to be a blush of embarrassment but no, arousal coursed through her veins. Faith shook her head. It seems she couldn't get enough of him, and even if he was sending her home she wanted more.

Crag froze and sniffed the air. He turned looking at her. A gleam once again shown in his eyes. He ran his head along the top of hers sliding it down her neck. A sensuous caress sending shivers down her spine. His tongue flicked out teasing her, electrifying her nerves, flicking the tips of her scales on the underside of her neck. Faith had no idea that it would feel so good.

She moaned. Surely, they had time for one more roll in the hay, so to speak.

We need to get going.

Faith blinked surprised at the unknown voice in her head. She looked at Crag in question.

That is my sire. We need to go back. He flicked his tongue against her neck one last time smirking while she shivered. *We will finish this later.* The gleam in his eye assured her of that. His head butted her lightly, herding her toward the door.

I'm going. You don't have to push. Swishing her tail, Faith snuck around him. She heard Crag chuckle behind her. Faith tossed her head, sniffed and stalked back to the large room where the dragons surrounded the hatchlings.

Faith stopped in the entryway to the large cavern causing Crag to trip into her. An amazing site greeted her eyes. She looked around, dumbfounded. She had no idea there were so many dragons in the world. She shook her head, eyes rolling. Just a few days ago, she had no idea there were dragons at all.

The many bodies warmed the room. If it hadn't been so crowded the heat would be wonderful. She stood there looking in when Crag got pushy again and shoved her gently into the room with his head. He flicked his tongue against her, tasting her, making her jump. Faith glared at him.

Mmm, if you don't move, I will make a meal of you. Crag had a wicked grin on his face. He crowded her, forcing her to move. *Of course, I would prefer you stand your ground.*

A tail swatted Crag across his side, setting Faith to giggling. His dam stood there glaring at him. Crag rubbed his face against his dam's, laughing at her expression. He then turned and herded Faith further into the room.

Crag wound his neck around Faith's.

The hatchlings crowded around her. A spark lit inside of her. Her emotions in turmoil. She wanted to keep the hatchlings safe. She wanted to stay with Crag forever. She could see plenty of adventures heading their way, if only he asked her to stay.

Crag looked down at her with pride on his face. Sniffing, she could scent the happiness of the hatchlings as they crowded around her. Beyond them, above her, behind her, Crag's scent also spoke of happiness and joy.

Faith herself, had never been so overjoyed in her life. This is where she belonged. The thought of Crag taking her home sent a pain stabbing deep in her chest. Faith tried to ignore it, focusing on the joy this moment was bringing her. She would savor it forever.

I want to stay here with the hatchlings until they're all gone. Did you want me to take you first?

Faith blinked her eyes in pain at the question. She wanted this to last as long as possible. *I will stay until all the hatchlings are safe. Then you can take me home.* She closed her eyes, unable to stifle her pain. She opened them to see Crag watching her in puzzlement.

He watched her and slowly replied, *Okay. I will take you last if you are sure.*

Yes, I am.

Crag ambled away, heading over to the large flock, no, clan, of dragons that towered over the hatchlings. They had their heads together and then disbanded. Faith couldn't hear what they said over the sound of the hatchlings as they purred. They probably weren't even using voices she realized.

Faith looked around at the little ones smiling. She settled on the ground. Her wings against her sides. She didn't know what else to do with them. Crag used his almost as extra arms. Faith stilled, lacking the coordination to move wings and feet with the little ones pressing close. She didn't want to injure any of them. Faith settled completely on the ground and the hatchlings crowded her, maneuvering so as many as possible were touching part of her.

She sighed. She would happily prolong the feeling of joy that surrounded her. Crag looked over at her and she could feel the pride from him wash over her. She couldn't help but hope that her future was with him and not back home with her family.

She was confused. This was all so new to her. He couldn't, wouldn't, turn her into a dragon and leave her. She hoped and prayed. He called her his mate. Not knowing twisted her stomach. She swallowed the nausea rising inside. Taking a deep breath, Faith reminded herself that she could ask him. There was no use in worrying about it, until or when, her fears were realized.

She looked around the cavern. Many of the adult dragons were leaving in pairs and each carried at least one of the hatchlings with them. There were more than she had originally thought. Pandemonium, orchestrated chaos perhaps, surrounded her. The flurry of movement in contrast to the moment she first stepped into the cave.

It cheered her up. Hope swirled, where before death and hopelessness tore it away.

She needed a bit of her name. Faith. A life that she never imagined beckoned to her. She wanted adventure and received more of it than she ever could have desired. Going back to the village, living back home, and the day to day drudgery became unimaginable.

Faith gasped, the air in her lungs strangling her. No. Faith lifted her head, drawing a deep breath. Just keeping breathing, she told herself. Ask him what he intended. Surely, she was getting worked up over nothing. She just needed hope. The cavern was filled with it.

She needed to focus on the situation around her, not something she couldn't do anything about right now. She looked around her. She wouldn't give this up for the world.

She waited, the group of hatchlings getting smaller and smaller around her. The dragons taking them out one by one. She noticed some of the larger dragons that had left earlier were back. It couldn't be too far away; this lair Crag spoke of. It had been hours, her sitting here worried over her fate.

Crag and his siblings glided back in, following at the rear of the group. Loading the rest of the hatchlings on dragon back, the cavern emptied out. Crag and she were left alone.

His eyes locked with hers and he came toward her, shifting as he did so. Faith looked at him and unconsciously shifted too. She stood there and admired him. His black hair soft as silk to her touch. His broad shoulders tapered down to rock hard abs that led to a mouthwatering glory trail that arrowed straight to his straining cock.

Faith sucked in her breath. Her breasts tightened, her nipples hardening. Her stomach quivered in anticipation. Her sex softened and dampened in preparation, aching to be filled.

From the flair of Crag's nostrils, he could tell. He stalked toward her. The stark desire on his face made her passage tighten, clenching on emptiness.

She needed him. Forever.

Crag reached her and grasped her waist in his hands. He lifted her and thrust his pelvis forward. Bringing her down, he speared her fully on his erection.

Faith shattered. Her pussy quaking on his hard cock. He stood there boldly, legs locked to keep himself steady, lifting her up and down. Forcing her to ride him at his pace.

Faith wrapped her legs loosely around his hips. Her body quivered, loving the thrusts piercing her body. Shivering from the sensations of him gliding against her inner walls. She clutched Crag against her, satisfaction filling her at the feel of him inside her. Each time he withdrew, she moaned. With every thrust deep into her, she gasped. Each cell of her being grasped him, wanting to absorb his soul into hers. The warm heat of her pussy tightened in excitement. His hardness massaging every nerve ending. Her body sent rush of cream to coat them both.

Crag caught a nipple in his mouth.

Faith's breath caught.

He suckled in rhythm to his thrusts. Pulling his head back, he let her nipple slide out with a pop. Flicking it, he then attacked the other, giving it the same treatment.

Faith tightened on him with each suckle, her blood heated, unable to catch her breath.

Crag rammed into her with short, sharp bursts. Faith tightened, breaking. Tossing her head with a scream, Crag backed her into a wall, holding her in place. He thrust rapidly inside her, jackhammering her without mercy. One hand grasped a breast, pinching her nipple. The other slid sensually down her sensitive tummy, grazing her clit.

With her body shaking, she choked back a scream and, shattered on him. Her body milking his cock until he exploded inside her.

Crag pumped, with each thrust his cock swelled, shooting warmth into her willing body. She accepted the warm spray of cum, clenching him inside there. They stood there, her back against the rock wall and her arms limp over his broad shoulders. Sweat rolled down her temples. They were both a mess, drenched. Their heat sizzling even in the cold air.

Faith could feel him still deep inside her. Each throb of his penis answered by her pussy clenching to keep him inside. Even the stone wall of the cave didn't matter. Only the throb of him joined with her.

She crossed her ankles, determined to keep her legs wrapped around his hips. One of his hands shifted to cradle her ass, his fingers brushing where they joined, teasing her asshole, sending a shiver to her toes. His other hand slowly petted her pussy, running along her lips and then settling on her clit. She tightened, enjoying his delicate strokes. His callused fingertips adding just the right amount of roughness. She'd never get enough of him.

She stretched her body, luxuriating in satisfaction. Rubbing her nipples against his firm chest, they tightened. Peaking against the luscious feeling of his warm, hard body. Faith sighed with pleasure, tightening her core on him, his strength adding to her thrill.

He was steel inside of her, hot, hungry, and throbbing inside her.

Face undulated on him, gasping at the sensations zinging along her sensitive nerve endings.

He teased her clit into a peak. Dipping his finger down, tickling her, sliding along where they were joined. He slid it back and forth, tracing a slick path back to her clit. Faith jolted at the sensation. Her breathing deepened, the sensations washing over her. Goosebumps rose along her skin.

Crag rubbed his callused fingertip harder on her clit. Thrusting in and out, the slickness of her pussy easing his way.

Faith adored the fullness inside her. Her chest heaved, sucking in needed air.

Crag quickened his pace. He pressed her into the wall. His breathing changed, the wildness of his Dragon coming to the fore.

Faith could see it, gazing into his eyes. She could feel it in the hardness, the additional fullness of him sliding forcefully in and out of her. He roared, pinning her against the wall. Faith shuddered, tightening, breathe catching from each of his thrusts. Bursts of cream warming her insides. Fireworks exploding behind her eyelids. Exhaustion claimed her body.

They shuddered together, exhaling. Tingles shot through her pussy with the jerking of his cock as it emptied inside her.

Crag laid his head on her shoulder, shaking.

They stood there, his weight holding her upright. Both leaning for support against the rock wall of the cavern. Their breathing slowed and Crag pulled his head back. He looked down at her and smiled.

"I'll never get enough of you." He punctuated his remark with a kiss. The taste of him melting Faith's insides. The sensual feel of his lips pressing against hers. His tongue tangling with hers in a slow dance sent her heart skipping.

He lifted his head, his eyes smoldering.

"I love you." Faith boldly stared into his eyes.

A look of satisfaction entered his eyes, making her insides melt. Crag kissed her again his hands coming to rest at her waist. He stepped back lifting her off of him. She felt a sense of emptiness, emphasized from the warmth of their joining seeping down her leg.

"Are you ready to go?"

Faith stilled at his words. Did she read him wrong? She looked down at the floor, unable to continue gazing into his eyes. She didn't want to see the finality she knew she would find. She nodded.

"I didn't figure you would want to leave naked, so I brought clothes."

Faith peeked at him, confused.

Happiness lit his face.

"Thank you." She whispered barely able to get that out. A crushing sensation filled her chest, fighting with hope. Why did she tell him she loved him? Why did he have to look so happy at taking her home?

Crag's hand lifted her chin up until she was staring into his eyes. His fingers firm on her jaw. He frowned, confusion filling his eyes.

"Faith, what is the matter? Did you not want to go home?" His voice was low, almost as if it pained him to say that, as if afraid of her answer.

"No, I don't want to go home." She swallowed. The burning sensation in her eyes letting her know that any moment she would be unable to keep them from spilling down her face. "I want to stay with you."

Faith lowered her head, wanting to sink into the floor. She had not meant to sound so needy. She wrapped her arms around her waist, hugging herself. Conscious to her toes of her nakedness.

He tried to raise her face.

She resisted the pull of Crag's fingers. She didn't know how she could look at him, knowing that he didn't want her forever. She peeked at him from beneath her lashes.

"Faith." There was an urgency in his voice she didn't expect. "I promised I would take you back to your father so that he knew you were okay." Crag shook his head, a shit eating grin crossing his lips. "But I never planned on leaving you there. Not from the moment I realized my heart was in your hands."

Faith whipped her head up. Her heart bursting with hope. "Do you mean it? You want me?"

Crag smiled down at her. "How could you doubt it? My fate was to find you." He pulled her against him. "I love you. How could I not want you?" He chuckled. "Didn't I just show you how much I want you?"

Faith threw her arms around him, her escaping tears now ones of joy. "I love you, too."

"Then come home with me, my fated heart." He kissed her, his sensual touch a promise of their future together.

THE END

About the Author

Beverly Ovalle dabbled with writing on and off for years when her best friend finally dared her to submit a story to a writing contest. Beverly decided she had nothing to lose and since she'd always wanted to be an author sent it in and agonized for months waiting to hear back. Contract in hand she has never looked back.

An avid fan of all romance, Beverly's goal is to share her love of the written word and write the hot and erotic romances that she enjoys. She writes what she loves to read and it was only a matter of time before her obsessions crept into her writing for her to share. She hopes you enjoy her tales as much as she loves writing them.

A Navy Veteran, Beverly has traveled around the world and the United States enabling her to bring her settings to life, meeting and marrying her husband of thirty years along the way for her own romance. Reading romances since the fourth grade she's followed as the genre changed and spread into the vast cornucopia of romance offered today.

Other Books by Beverly Ovalle

Dragons' Mate

A Dragon's Treasure

Rise of the Dragons (prequel A Dragon's Fated Heart)

Stealing Hope (A Dragon's Fated Heart book 1)

Touched by the Sandman

Lighting Strike (The Glen book 1)

Willow's Cry (The Glen book 2)

A Saint's Salvation (The Santiago's book 1)

A Sailor's Delight (The Santiago's book 2)

Love Me Forever

Triple D Dude Ranch

Made in the USA
Columbia, SC
26 May 2019